PRAISE FOR
Mademoiselle le Sleuth

"Ready, set, encore! Tuohy has done it again. Sarah and her beloved cast of colorful characters are back to reprise their roles in another theatrically enchanting murder mystery set, *bien sûr*, in the City of Light. Hold onto your chapeaux. This is one fast-paced whirlwind of a caper."
— Nina Solomon author of *Single Wife* and *The Love Book*

"Colorful characters and laughs as well as scares abound as an American actress and her 4-year-old niece find themselves in the crosshairs after two brutal murders. The duo roams the neighborhoods of Paris, sometimes veering off the grid as they search for answers at the morgue and the cemeteries where Baudelaire and Sarah Bernhardt are buried."
— Kay Williams, author of *The Matryoshka Murders* and *Butcher of Dreams*

"Theasa Tuohy's four delightful female ex-pats score another victory over mysterious dark forces in the City of Light."
— P.M. Carlson, author of the Maggie Ryan mysteries

Mademoiselle le Sleuth

THEASA TUOHY

France House Press

MADEMOISELLE LE SLEUTH by Theasa Tuohy

Published by FranceHousePress

First Edition November 2024 

Copyright © 2024 Theasa Tuohy

Author Services by Pedernales Publishing, LLC.
www.pedernalespublishing.com

Library of Congress Control Number: 2024911963

ISBN: 979-8-9850771-3-1 Paperback Edition
ISBN: 979-8-9850771-5-5 Hardcover Edition
ISBN: 979-8-9850771-4-8 Digital Edition

10 9 8 7 6 5 4 3 2 1

Printed in the United States of America

With many thanks to *editor extraordinaire* Cameron McDonald and to all my friends who I have turned into characters. And, as always, my writers group.

In those happy days before
Notre-Dame Cathedral burned and Paris streets
became thick with electric scooters.

CHAPTER 1

Miranda had on her best dress, not her Lady Gaga T-shirt. Her mom had demanded it, even though the kid fancied herself a detective. It was showtime. Vicki bent down to adjust the big satin bow topping her four-year-old's fluff of blonde curls.

"No pouting. No jeans. You insist on coming to the opening of Aunt Sarah's show instead of staying home with a babysitter, so you know the deal."

"The show must go on. I have to be there."

Vicki's flicker of a grin was all but imperceptible. She shook her own angular, dark bob. Where did this show-off kid, her polar opposite, come from?

"Okay, bud. Let's roll."

The show must go on. Vicki fervently hoped so. Rehearsals, off and on for weeks, had made it hard for her sister to pick up Miranda after preschool. With Vicki's impossibly unpredictable schedule as a reporter and her husband so often away on foreign assignments, it was urgent that they have a dependable babysitter. But scatty Sarah, who'd only recently arrived in Paris and didn't speak French, always brought chaos no matter what country she was in.

Her involvement in this play had already landed her American ex-pat family and friends into international intrigue and murder. Although she could hardly be blamed for the tragedy of a fellow actress's murder, she could be blamed for insisting that such a shaky, low-budget production be kept going. Sometimes it was tough to tell who was younger, her precocious child or her adult but mercurial sister.

Vicki patted goodbye to Chess before closing the big Parisian-blue front door. She smiled, as always, at the irony of its attached sign, *Chien Méchant,* Mean Dog, warning evildoers away from their sweet-tempered golden retriever.

Miranda reached on tiptoes to call the elevator, taking charge of what she saw as her inalienable right to punch any button, turn any key that came within her purview. Her patent-leather Mary Janes tapped in excitement as mother and child passed through their interior courtyard, out the big oak door to their tree-lined street, and headed for the metro.

They were way ahead of schedule — Vicki had left the newsroom early to pick up Miranda at school — so they got off at Châtelet for a leisurely walk to the theater, some distance into the ancient quarter of the Marais. As they made their way through traffic, crossed the busy intersection, and passed the Sarah Bernhardt Café, Miranda piped up, "That's where Aunt Sarah buys me ice cream."

When they reached the Hôtel de Ville, early as it was, its fountain waters already danced in the lights playing on the magnificent old building. On good days, dusk stays long in Paris, but barely into September as it was now, evenings stretched way into the night.

Passing the shuttered merry-go-round, Miranda said, "That's where that bad man pulled me off the galloping horse."

Vicki laughed, not at the terrifying memory, which she'd tried hard to push from her mind, but at her repeated attempts to get her imaginative child to make the distinction between the thrill of a gallop and the up-and-down motion of a carousel steed. It was a question of correct language, not living in a movie like her sister.

They passed the grand BHV department store, headed up the rue Vieille du Temple, and took a right at the cobblestoned alleyway leading up to the theater.

A low hum of anticipation rippled through the audience. A group of early arrivals had saved them seats: Vicki's Irish friend, Mary Laughlin, and the dashing cop she'd met during the previous mayhem, who they all now referred to as Mary's detective. Sarah's housemate and best friend from college, John, and his partner, Ben, were in the row just in front. Vicki glanced around. A few people still coming in, no doubt a full house — all that advanced hoopla about the murdered actress. Who, to top things off, had turned out to be some kind of British spy!

"A marketing guy's dream," Vicki quipped, as she sat down next to Mary. Certainly so, she thought, for a small production in a tiny theater stuck off behind an old rabbinical shop-turned-disco in a back street of the Marais. And in English yet, for a Parisian audience. The place was packed with reporters; she spotted several she knew. All anticipating something awful. The British tabloids had had a field day: FROG CRAZY STALKS UK ACTRESS. That was probably her favorite, although A ROLE TO DIE FOR wasn't bad.

To Vicki's journalistic mind, DEATH TAKES CENTER STAGE seemed more like the title of a play.

"I hope they can finally get this thing up and running,"

John said in greeting, turning in his seat. "I don't know how poor Sarah could tolerate any more disasters interrupting this production."

"God help us, none of us could," Mary replied.

Miranda settled in with a phone video game — her bribe for good behavior — was happily swinging her legs back and forth, her little feet not touching the floor. *Let's hope it stays this way*, Vicki thought. It had been a losing struggle to keep her strong-willed child from coming. She wasn't about to be left out of opening-night festivities. After all, her favorite — and only — aunt was the star, and Miranda was not about to be deprived.

"We're detectives together," she'd insisted, "and I need to see the show. If something happens, I can look for clues." As preposterous as that seemed, the kid and Vicki's clever but ditzy sister had recently unearthed information that helped Paris police jail a bevy of crooks and solve the mystery of that actress's murder.

Miranda's reward to herself, after a chief investigator dubbed her "the Eloise of four-year-old detectives," was to stretch her age. She'd now taken to informing people that she was four-and-a-half-and-three-quarters. She didn't seem to grasp the concept of almost five.

A spindly French youth in shiny pointed shoes appeared in front of the curtain with the admonition to *"Faites attention, s'il vous plaît, et éteignez votre mobile."*

"I want to finish my game," Miranda grumped. "Why did he say turn it off?"

"Because your phone would distract the actors. Now do it," Vicki commanded.

The curtain rose to reveal five people, one of them

limping away through a back exit to the slight thump of what sounded like a cane.

"Oh, there's Aunt Sarah," Miranda whispered excitedly. She'd been warned not to talk during the play. That whisper was loud.

"Shush," Vicki hissed through clenched teeth.

The scene was a restaurant, Sarah, at a small bistro table near the front. She was fidgeting with something, probably a fork, and kept glancing around. Vicki wondered why her sister wasn't looking at Ian Sommes, the blandly handsome, sharp-faced fellow seated across from her who played her husband, John. Same character name as Sarah's housemate, so the same-name-thing had given Sarah plenty to get upset about since John dies in the play. With her wild imagination, she'd kept fretting that friend-John would suffer the same fate as play-husband-John — getting stabbed to death by a dwarf.

Oh, the trials of a scatty sister. Vicki touched the real John on his shoulder and whispered in his ear, "That's you."

John nodded a silent yes and patted her hand.

But Sarah kept peering around at a table at the back of the stage where an elderly woman sat hovered over by a waiter with a towel on his arm. Well, the play was called *Don't Look Now*, so those nervous glances must be in the script. But why had the other limped off just as the curtain rose? There were supposed to be two elderly women. That was the idea, right? One was blind and psychic, used a cane. Yet a solitary woman sat at a table for two, twisted in her chair looking off to her left. Something red and shiny resting on the empty chair. Vicki knew all these arcane details because it was only a few weeks ago that the original blind actress was murdered. Was her replacement having a fit of stage fright? They all looked tense and displaced, a vapor of fear rising from the stage.

The unsettling silence lengthened. Someone in the audience coughed, the actors rigid in their places. Loud yelling erupted from backstage. Vicki grabbed Miranda's hand, but the kid was wide-eyed with anticipation. Jean-Louis Vidal, Mary's detective friend, sprang up one seat over and headed for the steps leading to the stage. Catching Mary's startled look, Vicki said, "Oh boy, what now?"

More yelling rolled out amid crashing sounds of a fight. The flat at the back of the stage swayed, the actors exchanged frightened looks, and the curtain abruptly fell.

CHAPTER 2

Sarah's bistro chair crashed to the floor as she leapt to her feet, heart pounding, to rush from the stage. This production had been cursed from the start. Worse than "The Scottish Play." Real people died. Who could be next?

A scream pierced the air. The lights went out. Someone grabbed her arm, and now she was the one screaming, trying frantically to jerk away. But Ian Sommes hissed in her ear. "It's me. I'm trying to help."

The stiff Brit had always seemed a rather weak reed, but Sarah was more than willing to follow his lead as they stumbled toward the back exit. The fright-filled voices of fellow actors rang clear even over the hubbub from the audience — did they think this was part of the script? There should have been five people on stage. Why on earth had Georgie left her chair for the curtain rise on opening night? It's a jinxed role. Jane Forsyth was thrown from a train, now her replacement does the inexcusable and walks off.

"If we shadows have offended," Sarah began mumbling to herself, hoping to throw off any curse. But this show wasn't even Shakespeare, much less the accursed Scottish Play. Why would the witches care anything about this eerie little offering from Daphne du Maurier?

As Sommes guided her through the back flat, Sarah stumbled over production cables, regained her balance, and again recited her token, "If we shadows," just as the lights were restored.

Gomez, the Brit director, a German with a Spanish surname, was close to hysteria — his usual mode. "Vhat haff appended? Vere is Georgie? She is replacement, but not here," Gomez lamented as he headed down the spiral staircase to the basement dressing room.

Pierre, an adorable member of the French crew — a favorite of Sarah's with his rust-colored hair and interest in helping with her French — moved to her side. "Gomez, he says same about Georgie before lights disappear, always the same with him."

"Who screamed? What's going on?" Sommes demanded.

Pierre shrugged. "*Le* lighting guy is not good. Never he was."

"But someone screamed *before* the lights went out," Sarah countered. She grabbed the stage manager, an atypically big-hipped French girl with nerdy glasses, shoving her way through to make an audience announcement.

"Did you scream?"

"*Non.*" The girl shrugged off Sarah's arm.

Another scream, this one a keen, rolled up from the basement.

"That's Gomez. He's found Georgie. We're cursed, for sure." Sarah started for the circular stairs, rattling off incantations as she went.

She found the director, his squat body braced against the

dressing room doorframe, blood smears on the white of his shirt front, moaning, "Ach, vhut horror, vhut horror."

She pushed past him, and there was Georgie, covered in blood, her head resting atop crashed bottles on the makeup table, a knife hilt glistening through the congealing red glob on her back. The bulbs circling the mirror were a constellation of small spotlights illuminating the grisly scene, blood and makeup running together down the walls and puddling across the floor.

"In blood, stepp'd in so far," Sarah cried, backing off in terror. Poor, dear Georgie! Both of us hounded by the curse of The Scottish Play. "If we shadows have offended," she intoned as she peered closer.

The knife looked familiar, exactly like the stage prop that the dwarf was supposed to use. But this thing was real. She eased in for a better look, careful to avoid stepping in blood. Good grief, it was the same knife, she could swear to it. But that wasn't ketchup slowly dripping from Georgie's body down her chair and onto the floor. Oh, Georgie! Brief candle. One that was a woman, but rest her soul she's dead.

The kid in the pointy shoes had just returned to the front of the drawn curtain when he was shoved aside by a woman in horn rims. *"Faites attention, s'il vous plaît. Nous avons un petit problème."*

"A little problem," Vicki said to John. The woman droned on about how to get a refund or return another time. Audience members began rising, muttering, and speculating.

"Where is the show?" Miranda demanded.

"Afraid not tonight," John said. The audience was on the move now, en masse, pushing and shoving, panic on the build.

John bent to pick up Miranda. "I'll get you to the door, then you and Mom go for ice cream. I'll check on Sarah."

"No, I'll check!" Miranda clearly could tell she was about to be left out of something.

Mary intervened. "Let's head for Sarah's favorite hangout. We'll save a table. She can meet us there."

Vicki took Miranda from John. "Good plan. Come on, little kiddo." Her voice left no room for argument.

Vicki, Miranda, and Mary were filing out, jostling along with the rest of the cranky crowd, Miranda still asking, "Where is Aunt Sarah? Where is the show?" when police arrived in force, armed and in riot gear, and herded everyone back inside. No one was going anywhere.

Sarah knew it was blood by its consistency, its smell. How did she know what blood smelled like? Fie, foh, fum. Fascinated, she reached her hand out ...

"*Arrêt.* DO NOT touch anysing."

She turned. It was the guy in jeans who everyone called Mary's detective. "It's Georgie. She's dead." Sarah immediately blanched. Pretty obvious, she admonished herself.

"Yes," said Detective Vidal. "I see. Please do not touch and go to help calm the players. Other police come *immédiatement.* You ladies bring trouble. Anoser one is dead."

"What do you mean ANOTHER?" Sarah demanded. "You mean this woman, right?"

Vidal shook his head. "Sorry. Is man upstairs who make the lights. He is tangled by the neck on a lever. The lights go up and down."

"What?" Sarah screeched just as the promised police

began crowding into the room. "By the neck? You mean hanged?"

"Yes. Now please to go upstairs. We must work this scene."

Sarah, climbing up, met John on his way down the spiral stairs.

"Too hard to hug you here," he said, taking her hand and leading her as he backed up to the top.

"Oh, sweet child." He grasped her in a bear hug. "I'm so sorry. What an awful thing."

"Mary's detective says the lighting man is hanged," she gasped into John's shoulder.

"Good god! Some kind of maniac is on the loose."

"The curse of The Scottish Play. I know, I played Lady Macbeth."

"Ah, babe. I know how much this show means to you. Someone seems determined to shut it down."

"I'm not going to let that happen!" She raised her head defiantly from John's embrace and swung a fist in the air. "But it makes no sense. Why would someone be killing people just to stop a show?"

"Come on, let's get you out of here. Vicki and Mary are taking Miranda to the Bernhardt bistro. Only way they could stop her from searching you out."

"Oh! Does she understand what happened?"

"Let's hope not."

CHAPTER 3

Sarah absently stirred her morning coffee, staring teary eyed at the pictures of her idol lining the walls of the Sarah Bernhardt bistro. This was her own favorite spot — a theater next door, another across the way. Folding glass doors thrown open to the busy Châtelet Square, presided over by a golden, winged woman atop a spiral column. Would she ever feel the same again? About acting, the theater? Nothing but escape and make-believe.

Last night was real life! Two people murdered, the theater a crime scene. Poor Georgie! She'd barely stepped into the role, learned her lines, and someone rips her life away. Didn't make any sense. What monster had it in for her? And the lighting man? A simple, sweet guy. Tall, skinny, not much English. Another Jean — all the French seemed to have the same few names. We never tried to talk, only smiled at each other. Was he an afterthought, a gruesome bonus for the killer? Sarah strained to recall what little she knew about the murdered actress from their work together last year — a brief run in London of The Scottish Play when Georgie had been brought in toward the end as a replacement. Poor thing, always the understudy. She'd mentioned a few gigs in the West End, her adored infant grandson. Perhaps a couple of ex-husbands.

Sarah shivered in the warmth of a gorgeous September day, the time the French called *la rentrée*. Miranda back to regular preschool, not the abbreviated summer classes, life renewed after the heat of a blast-furnace August. A new production for the fall season, would they ever get their show back up? Did she want to, after these grim reminders of the chasm between fantasy and reality? Gomez had been negative about their prospects. But did she care? No! She would move on to a *real* life. Work with underprivileged children! She stirred her coffee with purpose. Decided.

She smiled at a passing waiter. Then frowned. Yet what was she equipped to do, really? A poor player who struts and frets her hour upon the stage. That's all she was trained for. She'd end up clerking somewhere or selling shoes like out-of-work actors who used to peddle encyclopedias door-to-door. An image rose up, Sarah sitting on a Skid Row sidewalk, hand out, begging for alms. These words are razors to my wounded heart!

She brought the cup to her lips then slammed it down hard against its china saucer. To fear the worst oft cures the worst! She was good at what she did. She knew it!

I've scrabbled through the hard work of establishing myself — got an equity card, an agent. Damn it! I can't live with my feet stuck on the ground. The stage is my destiny. I've known that since I was five.

She had to continue perfecting her craft. She couldn't give up doing what she loved for teaching or something! How absurd. Do soldiers give up being soldiers when a comrade is killed? Of course not. Bernhardt always soldiered on when things got bad. Sarah looked up at an ancient poster of her heroine in field armor as *Jeanne d'Arc,* arrows piercing her body, and sat up straighter. She had to get a move on, get an idea, make plans to help herself. That's what Bernhardt would have done! Hadn't she turned the Odeon Theatre right here in Paris into a hospital when there was fighting in the streets. What war was that? Her world history was so sketchy, it was embarrassing.

But what now? Questions of where the cast could rehearse until the police finished up their forensics had pushed Gomez to the brink of hysteria. "Who vould take such a jinxed role? It has butchered two actresses," he'd yelled. After prodding, he calmed long enough to agree to a cast and crew brainstorming this afternoon at his rental apartment. How would the actors get paid? Was there any chance of using them in another project, etc.?

Sarah had insisted the meeting be scheduled late enough so she could pick up Miranda after school. Smiling again, munching her croissant as a waiter in a long black apron glided past, Sarah nearly laughed out loud recalling her sister's telephoned rendition this morning of her talkative, precocious child when the audience was being interrogated.

"It was a hoot, Miranda banging away telling the cops how she was a detective. They were bleary-eyed trying to hold her off. Thank heaven I don't understand French well enough to have caught what I'm sure were their sarcastic comments. Only good part about the whole thing was we were released before any of the other audience, obviously just to be rid of us."

But still another thing to fret about. Would a job with her own sister be enough to allow her to keep her visa? Some had assured her she needn't worry, that Americans could stay for six months without papers. Sarah didn't buy it. She'd gotten a work permit, so if the play folded, wouldn't she at least have to do a renewal or something? With all the warnings about French bureaucracy, she'd hate to tackle that. Especially with little French.

Where to begin? She looked up for inspiration at Bernhardt reclining seductively across a velvet couch.

Okay. First, she had to do something about learning French. How could she expect to stay in a country where she couldn't speak the language? She'd been able to get a proper American coffee this morning only because her sister taught her to ask for *élongé,* which came with cream in a big cup. If you just said plain old café, you'd end up with one of those bitty things of sludge so strong your head would blow off. She'd made that mistake once and had a buzz all day. My god, there was a lot to learn, if a simple cup of coffee was so difficult.

Second, she'd have to figure out how to look for a job. Pierre had offered to help her find crew work, but she wouldn't be able to manage the simplest stage gig for a French-speaking production. Google could help her find English-language actor groups, but however few there were could hardly offer much.

She pulled out her new cell phone and, with several false starts because she didn't understand the French prompts, began searching for language classes. But she found so many and was continually switching back and forth looking for English explanations, all of which were denoted by a British flag, not an American one, she finally decided to wait and get advice from friends on that quest. She switched to a search for theater companies but soon fell on something better — an American library. She knew there was an American hospital in Paris, but a library! Sounded swell. She'd go there and ask for help. She also figured she could find Bernhardt's autobiography there. That would give her inspiration, the strength to fight.

This was getting off track. She really had to focus on how to get *Don't Look Now* back up. But what actress would have the guts to take on a role in which two had died? Three grisly murders out of a small troop. Difficult to fathom.

Sarah desperately needed this show to keep going. She didn't want to leave Paris — loved it here, living with John and Ben, being near her sister and niece.

Gomez must be convinced to find a replacement! But who? Perhaps she should read the role, just while he searched. Of course, just for rehearsals. But that was totally ridiculous! Dangerous. Place herself upon a wheel of fire? In her agitation, she jumped up and declaimed to all in the bistro, "I fear I am not in my perfect mind."

The waiter came over with a perplexed frown. "*Oui*? More café?"

"No, sorry." She sat, then smiled up at him. "You saw us on the vaporetto. But not today. You saw us in the future." Yes! She knew all of Georgie's lines in the role of Heather, the psychic.

The waiter's frown deepened. "Tea? You want tea?"

Oops. Sarah shook her head. She had to quit saying what she was thinking. Mortified, she looked around. The coffee drinkers all seemed intent on their cups, or their cell phones. She settled back, peered into her own empty cup. If she believed that the show must go on, then she should make the sacrifice. Even if it put her own life in danger. But convincing Gomez that she could play an old lady, an elderly blind Brit — even in rehearsal — that would be the problem. Well, so what if people saw her only as the California blonde with a Valley Girl mentality? She'd show 'em.

CHAPTER 4

Sarah had Miranda by the hand as they passed one after another of the new, upscale boutiques and tea shops on the old, crooked rue du Temple, heading for the promised meeting. Gomez had given them all the building door code, and Sarah tapped in the numbers before remembering a four-year-old's insistence on being the one to punch, twist, or insert — any act necessary to open doors or start up contraptions. So, even though Sarah let her hit the elevator buttons, Miranda was still as squawky and cranky as the ancient cage that carried them up. "You didn't let me," she whined. "Mommy always lets me."

The apartment's door stood ajar, animated voices coming from within. Sarah needed freedom for a full-court press to argue for keeping the show running and, knowing that Miranda could be counted on to distract, grabbed the chance to sequester her pouting niece in the first room they passed in the long entrance hall.

"Brighten up, little kiddo," she said as she ruffled the blonde curls, handed over her cell phone, and told Miranda to have at one of her favorite games. The pout left, the sun returned. "I'll be just in the other room," Sarah said in parting. "We have serious business to discuss."

At the end of the hall and into the grand salon, Sarah was startled that the apartment was large and posh, with modern furnishings, yet ancient high ceilings and sculptured moldings. She looked around to see who of her colleagues were there, but their number was complicated by who was missing. The crew's situation was simple. The previous seven had been reduced to six with the death of the lighting man. The cast of five was diminished by the death of Georgie. There were two understudies, one for the two men in the cast, and one for Sarah's role of bereaved young mother.

Georgie had originally been standing by for the two older women, but when she stepped in for the murdered actress, no new understudy was hired. Everyone was here! So now there were six crew and six actors, plus the director. A shiver skittled across Sarah's spine. Thirteen was not a lucky number. She thought of Agatha Christie's *And Then There Were None.* Would all of them end up dead?

Who had done in poor Georgie? Attention was riveted for the moment on Rachel, who played the sister of the elderly blind woman.

"I just don't know what I saw," Rachel repeated in her Scots-tinged Brit speak for the third time. "How could I not, the police kept saying? You were seated just across from each other at a tiny table."

"Yes," said Gomez, "you must haft seen somezhing."

"One would think," Rachel replied, shaking her soft graying curls. "But it's a blur. My eyes were watering. Some smell caught my attention, I turned away to my left, and then just a blur when I turned back."

"Also," the bespeckled stage manager said breathlessly, "how you say, *un imperméable rouge,* as in *le* film."

"What?" Sarah demanded. "What was that?"

"A red mackintosh," Rachel replied. "On the seat where Georgie should have been sitting. Like the dead child wore in the movie of *Don't Look Now.*"

"Vell, all zat's for police. Ve haff ozzer problems." Gomez placed two bottles of wine and glasses on a coffee table and launched right in. The London producers had informed him that since they were obligated under contract to pay theater rent regardless of whether the show was running, they couldn't pay the actors unless there were box office receipts. Salaries for cast and crew would be paid for one more week, then that was it. They weren't working under a regular UK Equity contract.

The shouts and questions were immediate.

"How can we rehearse with the police still calling it a crime scene?"

"What's there to rehearse until we find a new actress to play the psychic?"

"Who in their right mind would take on that role? Two women have so far been killed."

Sarah was surprised that Gomez was not so volatile as when he was directing. But his conclusion was chilling: "Is clear. Ve try to keep going, or ve're all out of work." He stopped, seemed to suck in breath as he pulled a large handkerchief from his back pocket and wiped his balding pate. His hands were shaking. "And," he added, "vith murders, is it not too grim to go on? Replace the light man, ve can do. The actress. Difficult." To Sarah, that translated as The Show Will Not Go On. She was torn. Damn, she so wanted to stay in Paris.

"Well bother, don't these so-called producers have insurance to cover such a contingency?" demanded Ian Sommes. Her play-husband, with his stiff personality, often reminded Sarah of Jeeves, the butler — even resembled him, tall and thin with slicked-back dark hair — but he *was* making sense.

"They say no," Gomez replied. "For a British company, too much trouble to have a French policy. They must indemnify families of ze dead, but zat is anozer matter."

Sarah flared up. "Just who are these producers? Aren't they the ones who got us into this mess in the first place by allowing an undercover spy into the cast?"

Gomez flushed bright red as Sommes jumped back in. "That is indeed a good question."

Indeed, it is, Sarah thought. What kind of director would allow some producer from afar to cast an actor unknown to himself? She was nuts to think about taking on the death role in this ill-fated production.

"Yes," said Rachel. "What do you know about that, Mr. Gomez? An MI6 agent put in a role that ended up getting her killed! And left us to scrabble with an understudy."

To Sarah's amazement, Gomez didn't launch one of his famous tantrums. Instead, he gave a slight shrug to his left shoulder, as though to say it was none of his doing.

Sommes was adamant. "There is something fishy. Who are they? My agent had never heard of these producers when she sent me for the audition."

"To tell truth, I am not sure," Gomez replied. "I was referred by friend." He waved an arm to encompass his surroundings. "A sojourn in Paris." He shrugged, "Vhy not?"

"I auditioned you," he pointed to Sommes, "and Rachel. But Sarah already cast, and first dead actress, this Jane Forsyth or Blane Gowan, whatever ze name, was substituted at last minute for anozer zat I had chosen."

"Yes," countered Sommes, "by the Home Office. Right?"

A murmur spread through the room.

"Bloody hell," exclaimed Sommes.

Sarah glanced around at the stricken faces. "What do you mean? Like in the first go-round, we all were working for the British CIA?"

"Something akin to that. It certainly seems a possibility," Rachel whispered.

"Did you come through the Home Office, too, Sarah?" This from Margery, Sarah's understudy, the pretty blonde in a red dress lounging on the sofa, wine glass in hand.

"Certainly not," Sarah snapped. Margery always seemed to be gunning for her. Definitely wanted her out of the way so she could step into the role of the grieving mother. No doubt would get her vote, if Sarah were foolish enough to volunteer to read as the psychic. Get her bumped off, that's what would happen. "My agent sent me for a proper audition in Los Angeles."

The six French crew members had been following all this with deep frowns of concentration, clearly giving their limited English a heavy workout.

"*Que-ce que c'est*," Pierre finally exploded. "This is the same as *Sécurité Extérieure*?"

"Who knows what the French call it," said Sommes. "But the French word is pretty much the same: *espion*, from espionage, like our word."

"Ah," Pierre grinned, "so this is fun, *non*?"

"Maybe at your age," snapped Sommes. "I don't find it at all amusing."

"Well, we've got to do something," Sarah said. "It's a good play, and none of us can afford to be out of work." She grinned. "And look at this swell apartment, Mr. Gomez. You don't want to have to give this up."

He laughed, startling Sarah. She never remembered hearing him laugh before. The guy was apparently half human once you got him out of the theater. Or, a Jekyll and Hyde?

"I haff already made calls looking for Georgie replacement, but not luck so far. Demanding role, ve need English, age, and experience. Not an inviting prospect. Low pay, haff to move over here for short time ..." He trailed off.

"And the likelihood of being murdered," Sommes finished the sentence.

"Let's keep trying," Sarah said. "Faint heart, n'er won the day." Yipes, was she referring to her own cowardliness?

"I vill put to a vote," Gomez said. "Those who favor?"

All raised their hands except the stage manager. "*C'est n'est pas bon*," she said, rising from her seat. "With murder, *non*. I will take pay for one week."

Everyone stood and shook her hand. Gomez walked her to the door, said goodbye, then reaching for the doorknob of that first room off the hall, he turned and called back that he would make some phone queries. "I doubt can find an actress brave enough — or desperate enough for work — but vill try."

Sarah watched him go in and figured he would come back saying, "There is a strange small person in there." But when he didn't, she relaxed. Obviously, Miranda was too intent on her phone game to be a bother.

While they were batting around ideas of what to do next, the director came back, his face set in hard lines. "No luck."

Looking at her watch, Sarah was startled at how much time had passed. "Where's Miranda?"

"Miranda Richardson? She's not with us anymore."

"My niece?" Sarah leapt up and charged down the hall, her heart pounding. It was unlike the kid to not draw attention to herself.

The padded leather, yet sterile, office space was silent, blinds half drawn against the glare of the setting sun. Only the light from a computer screen glowed across the rust shag carpet.

"Miranda!" Sarah was frantic. Their lives had been in turmoil for weeks, almost ever since Sarah arrived in Paris a month ago to do the eerie English-speaking production. An attempt had been made not once, but twice, to kidnap the child because of a luggage mix up when she and her mother made a weekend trip to Prague. But that was behind them. The criminals were caught and jailed. Or were they? No! This couldn't be happening again! Miranda's school backpack sat askew, half falling off a beige ottoman.

"Miranda, please, oh my god, where are you?" Sarah screamed.

There was a rustle from under the desk, and the four-and-a-half-year-old crawled out, a grin on the cherub face.

"I was doing detective work. I listened to what that bald guy said on the phone. I think he was talking some different language. He's probably a spy."

CHAPTER 5

Thinking to dispel Miranda's notion of Gomez as a German spy, Sarah let her come sit in the grand salon, but with strict instructions that she could only listen. "You are not to talk. Understand?"

After exclaiming over what he momentarily mistook for a midget, Gomez found Miranda a glass of milk and a cracker before launching back into his lament about their problems. "Ve vere set up when producer allowed dot spy agency to dictate an actress. I haff been suspicious from the beginning. The first actress who plays the blind lady was hoisted on me."

"I think you mean foisted," snipped Sommes.

"Anyvay, I thought she was a relative, someone's mozer-in-law. But then ve find she was vith the spy bunch. So vhat is the producer up to? Who knows? But not good for show. Now ve haff a second dead actress. No good. Can't go on. Who'd take such a role?" He paced as he talked and pulled at his shirt collar as though he were wearing a tie that, in fact, wasn't there.

"I don't imagine that we will ever discern what MI6 was up to," Sommes said. "But..." His thin lips pursed into a sinister grin. "...it seems like an excellent way to blackmail the producer into keeping the show open. If word got out, he ran an MI6 front of some sort, it could ruin him. It would make a hell of a tabloid story. I can picture now how the *Daily Mirror* would handle it." He spread his hands wide and moved his head back and forth, arching his eyebrows up and down, as though reading a scabrous headline.

"Now," he intoned, "all we have to do is find some fearless old lady to take on the psychic's role."

"I'll do it." Sarah startled herself. She hadn't meant to say that. This role had a bull's-eye on it. She'd probably get killed just like the first two, but, damn it, if these guys kept messing around, she'd be out of a job on the next plane back to California.

"Yes," Miranda shouted, leaping off her perch on the couch.

"You hardly fit the bill, my dear." Sommes was almost sneering. "Despite what your sweet little niece thinks. And, I might add, it's curious, agent or not, how you secured the role you've got. After all, it *is* a British cast."

"She is vonderful." Gomez spoke up. "I vood be careful, if I vere you, Mr. Sommes."

"Quite," said Rachel.

Sarah drew herself up, the imperious queen. Lots of people thought she was a bit of a scatterbrain, but no one ever disparaged her talent. "I auditioned in Los Angeles. In addition to my New York agent, I also have one in London. I assumed she had recommended me." She didn't bother to mention that she wondered why they wanted an American actress. Even though she had done a school year abroad as a London theater intern, it wasn't as though she were a headline name, like a TV star or something.

"Margery, here, is standing by for my role." Sarah nodded at the grinning woman who obviously wanted her job, then mounted her breathless attack. "She can do the wife, at least to get us moving, and I can do the old lady. We could rehearse right here…" She waved her arm to encompass the spacious apartment. "…until the police release the theater. We could get the show up and running within a few days."

"All those lines to learn! And how old are you? Twenty-five, if a day. Heather is in her seventies. It's laughable," Sommes said.

Sarah drew herself tall. "I don't know about you, Sommes, but when I learn my lines, I can't help but memorize those of everyone with whom I interact. And just as you can, no doubt, I am able to play old or young." She paused. "Bernhardt played Hamlet, for heaven's sake. Any professional actor can do blind."

Gomez laughed out loud, and Rachel clapped her hands with glee. "Right on, my dear."

"Bernhardt," Sommes squealed. "You put yourself in her league?"

Gomez glared at him. "Is decided. Ve shall try. Report here tomorrow at 11." He abruptly stood up, unceremoniously dismissing them all.

CHAPTER 6

The unassuming little library was off on a side street a short distance from the Eiffel Tower, although the walk from the metro had taken longer than Sarah'd expected. She had to hurry. Mustn't be late for rehearsal. After her initial excitement, she was now having a case of nerves about playing an old lady. And rushing wasn't helping. But she must find some books about Bernhardt. How had she prepared for a role for which others felt she was unsuited? She'd played Hamlet, she'd done the nineteen-year-old Joan of Arc, for heaven's sake, when she was sixty-five years old! Sarah needed to get closer to inspiration than staring at pictures of her idol in a bistro. She needed substance.

Stepping inside, the library was like a warm embrace of home. Small-town U.S.A. — rows of book stacks, tacked-up notices of upcoming readings side-by-side with crayon drawings from kiddie events, a bank of computers for patron use, and an overly made-up woman who advised Sarah on local language schools. An ex-pat with American sensibilities but hardly sensible shoes like librarians of old. She was clearly a volunteer. She also identified the Franco-Prussian War as the time when Bernhardt had turned her theater into a military hospital. "Of course," Sarah said, trying to hide her ignorance. But gad, who knew?

She happily settled in at a table near the stacks with several books on Bernhardt and the war then remembered to check her watch. She had to get moving!

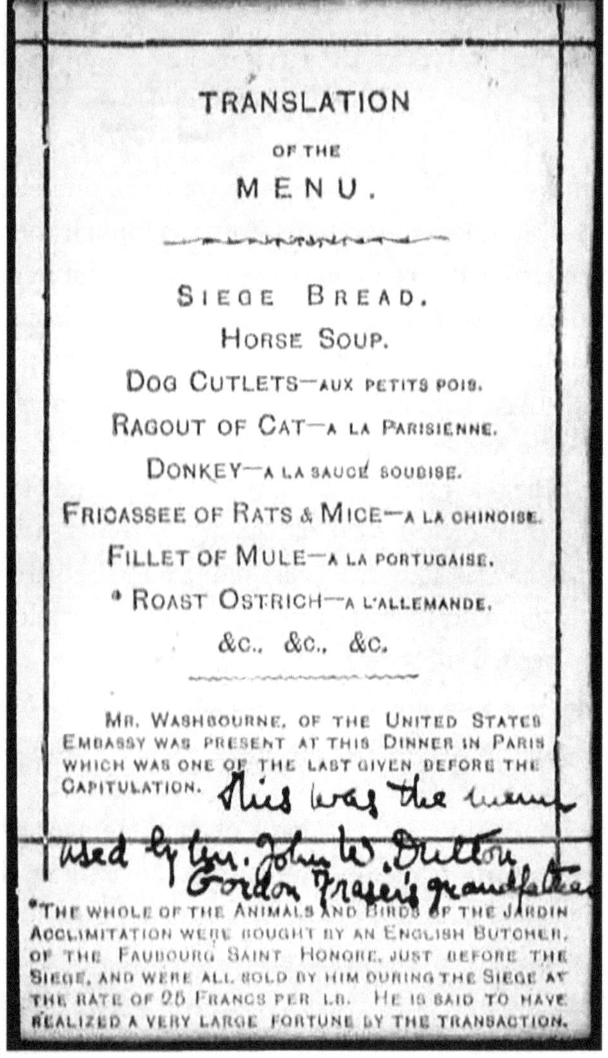

TRANSLATION

OF THE

MENU.

SIEGE BREAD.

HORSE SOUP.

DOG CUTLETS—AUX PETITS POIS.

RAGOUT OF CAT—A LA PARISIENNE.

DONKEY—A LA SAUCE SOUBISE.

FRICASSEE OF RATS & MICE—A LA CHINOISE.

FILLET OF MULE—A LA PORTUGAISE.

ROAST OSTRICH—A L'ALLEMANDE.

&c., &c., &c.

MR. WASHBOURNE, OF THE UNITED STATES EMBASSY WAS PRESENT AT THIS DINNER IN PARIS WHICH WAS ONE OF THE LAST GIVEN BEFORE THE CAPITULATION.

*THE WHOLE OF THE ANIMALS AND BIRDS OF THE JARDIN ACCLIMITATION WERE BOUGHT BY AN ENGLISH BUTCHER, OF THE FAUBOURG SAINT HONORE, JUST BEFORE THE SIEGE, AND WERE ALL SOLD BY HIM DURING THE SIEGE AT THE RATE OF 25 FRANCS PER LB. HE IS SAID TO HAVE REALIZED A VERY LARGE FORTUNE BY THE TRANSACTION.

Quickly flipping through, she was stunned by a restaurant menu featuring animals and rodents referring to the starvation of residents during the Siege of Paris of 1870-71 — horse soup, dog cutlets, ragout of cat, roast ostrich, fricassee of rats and mice? The French and their obsession with food presentation! Ragout? Fricassee? This can't be serious.

Sarah jumped up and stormed back to the librarian. "Is this true? And slaughtering zoo animals, too?"

The woman patted Sarah's hand. "Of course, my dove," her thick, almost black lipstick bunched into a dark oval, punctuating her face. Sarah snatched her hand back, startled. The volunteer label didn't quite fit with the black lipstick. The Bunuel classic *Belle de Jour* flashed in Sarah's head. But that wasn't a fit, either. Catherine Deneuve had a proper façade as a housewife who stepped out during the day. Turning on its head, the usual idea of a lady of the night.

Sarah slunk back to her books, chagrined at her lack of history and even more in awe of her brave Bernhardt taking a stand when the city was under siege.

Yes, here it all was. One of the oldest zoos in the world, established after the Revolution to incorporate the king's animals from Versailles. It was called *La Ménagerie*, meaning to take care of, and was in Le Jardin des Plantes. Stories of the time told the plight of two elephants, Castor and Pollux, favorites of Parisian children. Another tale: that Manet had eaten his own cat! Sarah decided she must go to *Le Jardin*, a huge park with the zoo in the middle. It would be an adventure for Miranda. Of course, no mention of the horrible, long-ago slaughter of the animals. Glancing through more books, she found a photo of Bernhardt's grave at Père Lachaise cemetery.

She returned to the little desk, to ask the librarian — it turned out her name was Tiffany — how to find the grave.

"Simple, my dove, there are online plot maps with numbers. Parisian cemeteries are great tourist attractions. Give me your mobile, and I'll upload one for you."

Sarah hurriedly bought a library membership, checked out several books on the celebrated French actress, including the autobiography "My Double Life," and vowed to explore, make a pilgrimage to the Comedie Francaise, the Odeon Theater, the Jardin des Plantes and all she could discover of Bernhardt's Paris. She must find some place other than a café with Bernhardt's name to feel closer to her muse. But right now, there was no time even for the metro. She had to grab a cab. Hectic day, first to rehearsal then pick up Miranda.

CHAPTER 7

Miranda was jumping up and down in excitement. "I love the monkeys the best. They play on ropes."

"How about the momma leopard and her baby?" Sarah asked. "Yesterday, you said they were your favorites."

"No."

Sarah sighed and pulled out the map she'd picked up at the entrance kiosk, but the forested paths just seemed to go in circles. "Not sure. What's the word for monkey?"

"Le singe. I like the thing that looks like a fox, but Daddy says it's a panda. He's black, and he's got red fuzzy feet." Miranda's tiny Mary Janes were tap dancing on the gravel, her blue hair bow bobbing. "Let's find him."

"You just said you wanted the monkey house."

"Le singe."

"Whatever, Miranda. What do you want to see?"

"Everything."

"Listen, I can't read this map. We'll just have to take what we get."

"Oh, look, there are those red things with the funny legs." Miranda was pointing.

Indeed, Sarah could see far down the path a green lawn

filled with flamingos. Half of them seemed to be standing on one leg.

Aunt and niece spent an hour moving from one animal to another, forgetting the map, taking what they could get. Sarah found it pleasant enough, but a zoo was a zoo. She was looking, somehow, for traces of Bernhardt. What a silly thing to expect! This wasn't 1870, after all, and thanks be, no one was eating zebras now.

They passed the momma leopard and her baby, and Sarah had to restrain Miranda from trying to crawl over the barrier.

"I'm getting tired, kiddo. Maybe we should call it a day. Tough rehearsal, lasted 'til just before I picked you up." Tough was hardly the word for it. Sommes kept sniping that Sarah was too young, Gomez kept comparing Margery's performance as the grieving mother unfavorably to how Sarah had played it. Pretty much a nightmare. Even so, they were making some progress.

"Just one more, please. Please," Miranda pleaded, "before we have cakes at the mosque."

"The what?"

"The mosque. We always get tea and sweets before we go home."

A thin, dark-haired young man in a pinstripe suit passing on the path stopped, bent to smile at Miranda. "The mosque, young lady. Did I hear you mention the mosque?" His English was strangely accented, but not with French.

"Yes, they have sweet goodies." Miranda's entire being seemed to dance.

"Indeed," he said, turning with a slight bow to Sarah. "Wonderful baklava. It's just up there. May I show you the way?"

"Thank you, monsieur, but that won't be necessary."

Before Sarah could restrain her, Miranda with hands on hips, had marched ahead saying, "I'm the leader. Follow me."

They climbed the paved path then the wide stone stairs before entering a patio with umbrellas opened over bistro tables.

Sarah, out of breath, turned to the young man. "Thank you, monsieur, it was very kind of you to lead us here."

"Oh, we need to sit inside." Miranda turned to their companion, clearly including him in her instructions. "It's better there."

Sarah tensed. The kid was irrepressible. Yet...might as well give in.

The room was cavernous, divided into varied sections by high Moorish arches of a rusty peach, the ceiling of painted patterns set between strips of light-blue wood. Bright colors everywhere, high curved windows bordered in violet, smaller windows inset with yellow and green stones and framed in aqua, banquettes upholstered in red and gold.

"Why do you call this a mosque?" Sarah asked, startled by the opulence. "It looks like a grand restaurant."

"It's part of a large complex for prayer and community activity," the young man replied.

When they sat, the three of them, Adeel was his name, the two adults chose straight-backed chairs at a tiny round table, passing up the large pillows on which a number of people sat cross-legged on the floor. Miranda perched on a huge tufted leather stool.

"Good heavens," was all Sarah could think to say.

"Oh, I've been here lots. Mommy and Daddy take me to the zoo lots," Miranda said.

She turned to Adeel. "We saw the red birds and the panda with the red feet."

"I've been here lots, too," he replied with a smile. "But I must say, I don't get to the zoo as much as I should. I surely would like to see that red-footed panda."

The waiter arrived, Miranda taking charge of which sweets they should order, then Adeel turned to Sarah. "And you, Mademoiselle, this is your first visit to the mosque?"

"I only came to Paris a few weeks ago."

"She's an actress," Miranda chimed in, "so she has funny ideas about things. She made me wear this dress. All the other kids wear T-shirts. But we're detectives together, so I do what she says. Besides, she's my babysitter."

Adeel grabbed his napkin to cover a laugh he turned into a cough.

Sarah grinned. "She's quite a talker."

He cleared his throat. "I'd say you are busy ladies. Detectives and an actress."

"I'm also her aunt," Sarah said. "How about you? Do you live in this neighborhood? Is that why you come here often?"

"Yes," he said. "I live nearby. I'm also a Muslim, with roots in Algeria. But shame to say, I come most often for the sweets, not for the prayers."

Glasses of minted tea and juice for Miranda arrived, along with a tray of sticky, date-and-honey-filled delights.

"So," said the young man, reaching for a cake, "are you in a show? English-language theater seems quite the thing in Paris at the moment."

"Ohm, that's a little hard to explain. I'm in a show that's been plagued by murders."

"Murders?" the cake, halfway to his lips, splattered honey

as he set it down hard on his plate. "*Mon Dieu*, this is the one that's in all the papers?"

"Afraid so."

"Do the police have any idea who's responsible?"

"I really couldn't say," Sarah said. Who was this guy, anyway?

"What a terrible introduction to Paris." Adeel's voice was warm, sympathetic. "The police here often have the reputation for — how you say in American TV shows — banging heads."

"They've been quite nice so far," Sarah said. "And it's been gruesome. We had two awful murders opening night, and an actress in the same role was killed before that."

Adeel leaned forward. "Surely you can't continue!"

Miranda, her face already smeared with sugar, piped in. "They are going to blackmail the producer."

Sarah laughed. "Miranda picks up things she doesn't quite understand. But, yes, I'm going to step into the vacated role, just for the moment. If someone doesn't do it, I won't have a job and will have to leave Paris. Sarah Bernhardt would have done it."

Adeel's eyes widened. "Really? Sarah Bernhardt?"

"It's not the CIA like last time," Miranda said. "But something like it. Do you know what that is?"

"I've heard of it," he replied, his eyes even wider.

CHAPTER 8

Mary Laughlin and Sarah watched the hearse pull up and back around to the concrete shelf where they stood. Mary had accompanied Sarah because the flighty greenhorn American would never have found her way to the Institut médico-légal, situated in a circle of mid-city exit roads from the motorway to Reims.

The family of the murdered Georgie was arriving from London for a viewing this morning before the body would be shipped home.

"I'm so glad you came with me, Mare. The rest of the cast said they'd show up, but they'll probably never find this place."

Mary had hinted more than once she hated that abbreviation of her name, but Sarah never seemed to retain the message. Apparently, the kid was great only at remembering stage lines. She seemed to have now gotten herself into a role that could kill because she knew everyone else's lines as well as her own.

"The guy who plays your husband should know. He identified the body, didn't he?"

"Yes, Sommes," Sarah replied. "A poor player who struts and frets his hour upon the stage."

"Should I translate that to mean that he's not your favorite person?"

"He's okay. He just picks on me," Sarah said. "But I still don't understand why we have to come to the morgue. At home, we'd go to a proper funeral parlor."

"That's how the French do it," Mary said. "Most bodies are brought here, and families can have services on premises if they like. With murder, of course, authorities are always involved."

Mary knew this drill only too well, having lost her husband Paul to cancer earlier in the year, and she'd been here again last month after Katja, Miranda's babysitter, was murdered. Mary still couldn't shrug off guilt for having proposed her dicey immigrant neighbor for the job. That's why she was here now. Trying to make some amends to Vicki by guiding her silly sister around. Mary's bonus for the agitation and disruption in all this was a budding friendship with the detective involved in that case. Her friends were all trying to imagine it a romance, but Mary's devastation at the loss of her beloved Paul couldn't allow for that yet. She'd left Ireland behind and turned her life upside down to become a French wife, her heart wasn't ready for new adjustments.

"So, does your boyfriend, the detective, know when we can get back into the theater?" Sarah said.

Mary laughed. "Anyone but you would ask what he knows about the murders."

"You would have said if he did."

Mary shifted her heavy handbag to her other arm, taking in the loading ramp atmosphere inserted into the middle of a tree-filled residential neighborhood. A green lawn spread from the red brick morgue at her back down to a highway along the edge of the Seine. Clusters of teary-eyed people stood around, awaiting their turn to be called in for a viewing. And two guys in jeans and leather jackets, off to themselves smoking, surely were cops.

"I'll go ask about Georgie. Maybe they'll know when the rest of her family arrives. They told me earlier, her husband is already here. In the waiting area." She waved her arm toward the dock walkway that ended in a large room resembling the lobby of a small-town train station.

"Husband?" Sarah replied. "I could have sworn she said she was getting a divorce."

"Interesting." Mary lifted her eyebrows.

"When we were in The Scottish Play together," Sarah went on, "he briefly played one of the three witches."

"Oh, you know him?"

"Not really. He was there for less than a day then got fired. Drugs, maybe booze."

"So, an actor, too," Mary said. "I wonder if anything can be made of that?"

Sarah shrugged. "Who knows? Maybe you should tell your detective friend. So, you never answered. Does he know when we can get back in the theater?"

Mary grinned, delighted to deliver the news. "He said last night that he thought the police were all but finished with it. I'd wager you'll be up and running by tomorrow."

Sarah's entire body seemed to brighten. "That's great. We did a book reading in Gomez's living room yesterday and have another as soon as we finish here."

Mary nodded toward a taxi, pulling into the paved area circling a giant chestnut tree. "Surely, now, that's Georgie's family."

The cab doors opened, and a distraught-looking middle-aged blonde emerged holding the arm of an older woman. "Brits, I'd wager," said Mary. "They look like they were dressed by Marks and Spencer."

Sarah stepped down from the dock and addressed the fading blonde. "Are you Georgie's daughter? She told me so much about you. I'm Sarah, and I'm so sorry."

"Thank you awfully." The woman gave her a tight smile. "I appreciate your meeting me here."

Sarah seemed to teeter for an instant on the ball of her foot, then settled back. Mary could see that even this young colt, who rarely curtailed her exuberant emotionalism about anything, had picked up a distinct vibe not to hug the woman.

"This is my friend, Mary Laughlin," Sarah said with an upward flick of her wrist. "The other cast members should arrive shortly."

The woman nodded. "This is my aunt, Martha Whittaker. Mother's sister."

"I understand someone is already here. Perhaps your father?" Mary said from her higher perch on the dock.

"My father! He's been dead for years." The woman, suddenly red-faced, was nearly shouting.

Mary started from the force of the words. "I'm sorry. Of course, I got it wrong."

The two women moved up to the walkway and marched ahead without another word. Mary called after them, "I think you'll find an attendant at the last door on your right."

Sarah turned wide eyes to Mary and shook her head. "What do we do now? Wait for the others or follow the Weird Sisters?"

"Let's mosey," Mary replied, "and see if we can sleuth out

what's up. You're the detective. The attendant already told me which viewing room they'd be using."

They watched the two women head for the waiting room at the end of the loading ramp then turn into a hall. As Mary and Sarah tentatively followed, they found themselves in a long corridor with a vegetation-filled outdoor space seen through plate glass on the right. On the left were what appeared to be small, chapel-like viewing rooms with stained-glass windows. They followed Georgie's relatives, keeping a good distance behind, then hesitated outside the room they'd entered. An angry explosion came from inside.

"How dare you come here!" a woman's voice shouted. "You're nothing but a rounder who used my mother to further your stage career."

Sarah tugged at Mary's elbow, nodding toward fellow actors just entering the long corridor and mouthed, "I'll head them off." She hurried down the hall, hands held up, palms out.

The cast and crew, all eleven of them, along with Gomez, registering various degrees of astonishment, stopped in the face of Sarah's urgent instructions.

"Daughter." Mary could hear her stage whisper from several dozen feet away. "Sharper than a serpent's tooth."

Mary had stepped aside, away from the open doorway of the viewing chamber. Out of which came as almost a flying projectile, a handsome — some might say beautiful — smartly dressed, middle-year man with touches of gray at his temples. His blue eyes seemed unfocused, non-seeing. But his face carried the bland, unperturbed serenity of someone enjoying a stroll in the park as he steadied himself, then glided past the cast of *Don't Look Now*, which had en masse moved to one side to let him pass. Mary didn't really remember much about Georgie except that she'd played a blind old lady. This bloke could certainly be cast as her son.

Mary moved down to join the gathered actors, but little was said beyond questioning whispers. This was, after all, a morgue. "Let's wait a few, to let the Furies calm down," Sarah said, then added, "Actually, he probably wasn't her father." Sommes crinkled his brows in a question, but the rest ignored the opaque reference to Georgie's daughter. "It's just like Bernhardt," Sarah went on. "A young husband she would always love. Jacques. He was a drug addict, too."

Sommes at his snippiest. "What are you babbling about?"

"That guy was briefly one of the witches in The Scottish Play." Sarah was as condescending as Sommes was snippy. "Georgie got him the job. But he was canned for being late to rehearsals."

At that moment, the woman, who had never volunteered her name, appeared in the doorway with a plastic smile and said stiffly, "You are Mother's friends? Won't you please come in for the viewing?"

CHAPTER 9

Sarah, breathless, turned the corner and, praise be, no tiny people swarming. She was on time! This business of rehearsals running into the afternoons wasn't easy. Gomez was grumpy and awful when she had to dash off, but when Miranda gets out of school, Sarah must be here. She had a school number she could call to alert them to keep the kid, but that was for real emergencies. Besides, with her lack of French, she had no way to explain a problem.

Awaiting the stampede of released children, she leaned against the metal rails separating the block-long school building with its French flag from the narrow street as she checked her cell for directions to the cemetery. She still wasn't sure about this.

To do or not to do? She desperately wanted to see Bernhardt's grave. She needed to keep her heroine front and center to get through this challenging role she'd taken on. She must continually replay her image of Bernhardt as Joan of Arc at age sixty-five — the audience roaring its approval when the great actress spoke the line "I am nineteen" to questions from her onstage inquisitors. Which was more difficult, to play it forward or backward? Neither was easy. It's a matter of sensing the part. But sometimes, it was a stretch to inhabit an infirm body and weary soul. And blind! How awful must that be? Sarah tried to imagine it, to keep her eyes closed. At one point, she had taped her eyes shut and bumped around John's apartment, trying to grasp that sixth sense.

But was today's plan a good idea? She wasn't sure Vicki would approve of a cemetery as an appropriate outing for Miranda. Perhaps she should tell her niece they were going to look at historical monuments. She knew the kid didn't understand the concept of death; it had taken her days after Katja was murdered to accept that her babysitter was gone. Miranda finally had decided on her own that it was the same as when her goldfish didn't swim anymore and just floated around their bowl belly up. Hard lesson for a small kid!

Miranda, laden with a book bag and still clutching her day's production of crayon drawings, was excited and skipping as they headed for the metro and a new outing, a new adventure. "I always like to look at monuments," she had replied to the proposal.

She was in the midst of rendering a blow-by-blow account of a boy named Michel pulling the hair of a girl named Regine when they passed the spot where aunt and niece briefly had been imprisoned in a van by the same people who had tried to kidnap Miranda. Sarah shuddered, but her niece was caught up in the more recent squabble in the schoolyard. Hard to believe that sizzling summer was only two weeks ago, now a new school season. A fresh new life, a challenging new stage role for Sarah.

Miranda chattered on as Sarah finally sorted out the best route by metro to the cemetery, carefully avoiding that word as she sought help from her niece with the occasional French direction.

They arrived at the grand gates opened onto a paved, tree-lined path beyond which Sarah could see a mélange of statues and monuments. She had seen pictures of Bernhardt's grave showing a heavy granite portico shading what appeared to be a coffin. Could the body really be above ground like that? The great actress had kept a white-satin-lined rosewood coffin in her home and slept in it from time to time. Few sources seemed to have a plausible explanation for that strange behavior. Although Sarah read someplace that Bernhardt had had the coffin since she was a sickly child, asking for it to help prepare herself for death. Perhaps that's what made her such an amazing, tragic actress, an endless sense of impending doom.

A caretaker stepped out.

"Tell him we're looking for Sarah Bernhardt," she instructed Miranda, carefully avoiding the word "grave."

Miranda had a short discussion with the man then turned to her aunt. "He says she's not here. She's with some priest called Lachaise."

"Not her heavenly resting place, just here," Sarah mumbled. How to rephrase without talking about death. She pointed toward the path. "Out there," she said in English and smiled at the guard.

"*Non.*" He shook his head. *"Père Lachaise."*

That was the name of another cemetery she'd read about. "But these are the directions the librarian gave me." Sarah was adamant, her tone defiant.

The caretaker shrugged, uncomprehending.

"We have to take another metro." Miranda frowned. "He

said lots of numbers. I'm not sure. It's across the city. This place is Montparnasse."

A deep silence ensued as a slight September breeze skipped along the path ahead.

"Here is good," Miranda said. "They have monuments too."

The caretaker handed Sarah a map — a bigger version of the one the librarian had put on her phone — a bunch of little squares with numbers. This strengthened Sarah's resolve to find Bernhardt's grave.

They started down the road amid a cheek-by-jowl hodgepodge of seraphs and sprites, veiled and grieving Madonnas, and tiny stone abodes that housed urns and stained-glass memorials. Graves were decorated by granite crosses, bas-reliefs, and busts, even some with elaborate avant-garde art.

Sarah, searching from right to left for site numbers, marveled. "I've never seen such a place. Cemeteries are nothing like this at home."

Miranda suddenly shouted, "Oh, there's my favorite thing." She was pointing at a huge white ceramic something or other with bright mosaic flowers and hearts all over it.

"You've been here before?" One never knew about this kid!

"We came one time to look at the statues of famous people."

Sarah laughed. "I don't think this thing is a person, Miranda."

"It's a cat."

As well it was, whiskers and all. A gigantic upright cat

that dominated the surrounding space with an orange and yellow daisy implanted in its ceramic belly.

But what to do next? "Let's look at this map the librarian gave me."

Miranda immediately tried to snatch the phone.

"Hold on a sec, little kiddo. I'll let you help. But I think we're on the wrong side of the cemetery." That woman, Tiffany, couldn't have been wrong about where Bernhardt was. She had pinpointed the site.

"See." Sarah handed her niece the phone and bent down to show her. "According to the markers, we're here and should be over there."

Miranda scrunched up her forehead, put her finger on the screen, moved it around a bit, and then handed the phone back. "My numbers don't go so big. We better do what the librarian said."

Sarah did her best to suppress a grin. "Thanks."

When they spotted an obelisk with the top half of a man, chin on hands, Miranda said, "Look. I told you it was statues of people."

"You're right. It has his name at the bottom. Baudelaire. He was a poet."

"He's the thinker."

Sarah laughed. "Not exactly."

"Yes. I remember. Daddy showed me."

"That's another statue, Miranda. You saw it someplace else."

"Maybe. But I remember Daddy called him 'The Thinker.' And he was thinking, just like this guy."

Sarah looked again at her map, bewildered. "This looks like the right number, the one she gave me. But nothing like the photo I saw. It had a coffin! What a dunce that woman was. I should have known! She was wearing those frivolous shoes."

She turned to Miranda. "They both start with a B. Do you think Baudelaire sounds like Bernhardt?"

Her niece eyed her for a moment then shook her head. "Mommy always says you say the strangest things."

"It's not me this time, damn it. She must have purposely led me astray. When she gave me the site number, she said, 'There, everything is order and beauty, richness, quiet and pleasure.'"

The startling bust atop the Baudelaire monument, high in the air, sported a full head of hair, bangs brushed off to one side. Elbows of the muscular arms rested on a column with extensions on each side that appeared to be angel wings. What looked like a wrapped mummy lay across the column's base. Who would expect a poet to have the arms of a wrestler?

Scattered all around, apparently from fans, were single stems of dead and dried-up flowers. There were handwritten messages, some on sticky notes, others on lined sheets torn from steno pads that were held in place by small stones. The few in English that Sarah could read appeared to be snatches of poetry.

"He makes *poésies*," said a man standing nearby. He wore a plastic bowtie on an elastic band around the collar of a clearly un-ironed shirt. His socks were as mismatched as his dress was unorthodox.

"He said 'poetry.'" Miranda, always on the lookout for ways to one-up her aunt on her lack of French.

"Yes, I know," Sarah replied to the man. Everyone around,

her niece, even this poor, seemingly demented stranger, always wanted to make her feel dumb.

"*Le Prince. Le prince des nuées*," the man repeated.

"I think we'd better move along," Sarah said to Miranda. She picked up the book bag her niece was dragging on the ground, took her hand, and hustled her back to the main road, looking back to ensure the weird guy wasn't following.

CHAPTER 10

Sarah arrived at the theater nervous, which was unusual for her. She had confidence in her professional abilities. But she had mouthed off about them to Sommes, and he had a point — there was a bit more to playing an old lady than a few pasted-on wrinkles and a shawl. Not to mention that she could be putting herself in the crosshairs of a crazed killer.

But here she was, frightened and excited at the same time. Their first day back in the theater since the murder and her first full-fledged rehearsal beyond book-readings. What a stretch for an actress. And what an exhilarating challenge! Gomez had agreed for the moment to these split rehearsals — early morning, then late evening — to accommodate Sarah's time with Miranda. Almost unheard of — just a symptom of the trouble he was having finding a replacement for two dead actresses. But a nightmare of juggling for Sarah, already wearing her out.

Gomez greeted her back in his harried director persona. "Are you ready? Ve must get moving. Ve don't haff all day. You say you know all the lines, ve shall see."

Why, Sarah wondered, does this guy's personality change so radically when he's not working? He must have terrible insecurities about his own talent. Or maybe he's just a perfectionist and working makes him nervous. Ah, who cares? He's the way he is. Still, it was strange his connection to those so-called producers.

As she wound down the spiral staircase, she remembered that awful sight from her opening night: Gomez, moaning, backing out of the dressing room, blood on his hands, his shirt, blood on the doorframe where he'd gripped it. Stepping over the threshold, that image burned, but Sarah steeled herself and walked in. She put down her handbag and script, readying herself for this new phase of her life, and looked over at the lights-framed mirror where Georgie's bloody head had lain.

Thank god, the place was cleaned up. And sitting on the dressing table's ledge, reflected in the glass, was a huge brass vase with jug handles, filled to overflowing with flowers — pink camellias, yellow roses, white daisies with dark-brown eyes — set amid shiny green leaves, a wreath of the same winding around the vase. Two palm fronds rose above the bouquet like waving flags. A three-by-five card was taped to the front with S A R A H lettered in red ink, a bit of which had run and streaked down the card to puddle on the counter.

She grabbed the card to see who had sent the gorgeous bouquet, but there was no envelope, no message from the sender. Who could it be? It must have been sweet John. Still, she shivered. The flowers were lovely, but the setting somehow felt evil, *Fleurs du Mals*. No, she must shake that. She had to work here!

"Places, everyone!" Gomez yelled, echoing down the stairs. Duty called! She had to pull herself together.

The actors spread out across the boards, Sarah moving

along with Rachel, who played her sister, Wendy. Sarah had put on dark glasses and, indeed, a shawl — that should help her feel the part. She lowered herself gingerly into the chair at the back bistro table where Georgie had so briefly been the last time they were on this stage. Creepy! Poor Georgie. And that awful daughter of hers. But what crazy thinking! She knew Georgie wasn't actually sitting here on opening night. All Sarah had seen when she looked back was the elderly actress as she limped off stage. The only thing in this very chair had been something red. Sarah leaped up with a screech. Blood?

"Vhat is it?" Gomez screamed. "Already you don't want za role?"

"Ohhh..." Sarah moaned, plopping back down. "I'm so, so sorry. I just remembered the opening night, and it scared me. It won't happen again. I promise." What a doofus. She knew Rachel had said it was a red mackintosh. And she, herself, had been through this several times with the cops.

I told them something red, told them Georgie never sat here. Why did she feel for an instant that she had? What was she trying to recall? Over and over, she'd told the cops what she'd seen. The killer's walk? Was it a glide? Vicki said she'd heard a thumping.

"Okay now," Gomez addressed Sarah, "if you please pull yourself togezer, you are Heather, ze blind lady. Blind. Remember. You are blind! And old and feeble. Margery, you are Laura, the young mozer full of grief.

"Run it," Gomez yelled. "Opening scene, a restaurant in Venice, Laura and John, dinner."

Margery and Sommes were seated stage front at another bistro table.

Margery began with her opening line: "Don't look now,

John, but those two English women over there have been studying us since we came in."

John: "Oh, for God's sake, Laura, can we give it a miss for once?"

Gomez screamed at Margery, "Zat is not right. You have to be more faces to your husband."

Margery shifted slightly toward Sommes and continued as Laura: "I'm afraid you'll have to admit that this time I'm right. They seem to want to make contact. One of them is on her way over here."

Sarah, carrying a cane, moved forward on Rachel's arm.

Laura: "No–wait–they're both coming. One is helping the other, who has a stick. Oh dear, it's not a walking stick. It's a white cane! The second lady is blind!"

John: "Please, Laura! I wanted a quiet evening, just the two of us. We're supposed to be talking to each other, dealing with our loss, not entertaining strangers in restaurants!"

Margery shuddered.

Gomez stopped them, yelling, "No, no. Margery, you are not registering subtle shock at ze word 'loss' as Sarah did. You have grotesque Halloween mask of a ghoul."

Sommes glared over at Sarah. Poor Margery just looked confused. *Yipes, everyone is going to hate me if he keeps this up*, Sarah thought, but as the blind lady she continued without pause: "We have a message for you. You must not be sad about the death of your daughter, Christine."

Rachel steps forward as Wendy: "Your little daughter, Christine, spoke to Heather," she tells the couple. "Things happen to Heather quite often. She is what one calls a psychic."

John rolls his eyes skyward.

"The little girl wears a red mackintosh," Heather adds.

Margery, in character as Laura, faints to the floor.

Behind her dark glasses, Sarah flashed on the dead child's red coat from the movie. Over and over, the floating image of that bright slicker. The red on Georgie's chair!

CHAPTER 11

John climbed the carpeted circular stairs and turned the big key, weary and vaguely troubled. Sales had been brisk in his little antiques shop. The sun had shone all day, rarer than one would imagine in often gray but always gay Paree. He'd had an invigorating evening walk around this neighborhood he loved. So, what was it?

Bisquit jumped and yapped "Welcome home." John scooped up and nuzzled the soft fur of the tiny spotted terrier. "Hello, sweet dog. Are you good? I'm happy you're here to greet me."

Yeah, I wish Ben were, he thought. Part of what was bothering him, he knew. His partner was so caught up preparing for his upcoming show that he salted himself away for endless hours in his studio down the long hall past their huge kitchen. Ben's bright abstracts adorned their walls, but lately, they seemed his only presence.

John flopped down heavily in a low living-room chair and surveyed his domain. God, he loved this apartment with its ceiling-high Parisian windows strung across the double salon fronting on rue des Archives, chock-full of precious mementos from his San Francisco home after his mother died. He'd met Ben shortly after moving to Paris and never looked back. Sarah was the main thread to his past life, the closest thing to family beyond Ben. John had mentored her at Berkeley, both of them in the theater department, he two years her senior. Now she was charging in and out with her stories of rehearsals and murders. It was a delight to have her here, especially with Ben so absent of late. But, as always, Sarah exuded chaos.

Since her arrival in Paris only weeks ago, his life had been in constant turmoil. First, her niece's suitcase ran afoul of an international sting operation, then the kid's babysitter was murdered and an undercover actress in Sarah's play was thrown from a train. Hard to blame Sarah for any of it, but John ended up caught in the vortex of the bizarre scenario. He'd hoped for some quiet for a while, get his old life back. Restore some calm. Instead, Sarah had taken on this role that somehow got two actresses murdered and might, yes, very well might, put them all in danger.

He lifted himself, bouncing Bisquit from his lap, and headed for the kitchen. First thing he saw was cheese laid out to aerate for the cocktail hour. Ben, so French, might neglect John but never the proper approach to food.

He pulled fresh veggies from the big side-by-side steel fridge and was washing them for crudités to go with the cheese when Bisquit let out a yelp and skidded across the tiles in a dash for the front door.

John dried his hands and was ready to greet Sarah with open arms as she and the yapping dog rounded the corner into the kitchen.

"How was the first day of rehearsal, *ma petite*?"

"Pretty fine," she replied. "I knew all my lines. So did

Margery, but Gomez kept ragging her to do the role more like me. It was embarrassing." She threw her right hand across her chest. "These words are razors to my wounded heart."

John shook his head. "You're such a ham."

"Yeah? Well, it's hard to figure Gomez. He's either a big ham, too, or something weird. He blows really hot and cold. We've all been saying — even nasty Sommes — that someone needs to approach him about being so harsh. That's no way to get the best out of actors."

"Right," John said. "All you artists are delicate."

Sarah cocked her head, a quizzical look. "Hmm. Maybe so."

"How about a glass?" John reached for the white wine he'd already taken from the fridge. "I could use a drink."

"Good idea. But what's up?" Sarah then answered her own question. "Ben, I suspect. He's been so busy."

John glanced up from pouring wine. "You're a mind reader."

"Not hard to figure. We barely see him."

"Barely see who?" Ben materialized in bare feet and paint-spattered jeans.

John and the room immediately brightened.

Sarah lifted her glass, "A toast to the artist's resurrection."

Ben gave them a sheepish grin. "Sorry to be so *occupée*, but I must make the work."

Sarah performed a gleeful little jump in place and clapped her hands. "You got that right. It's how we thrive. Right, Ben?"

He gave them another shy smile.

"By the way," Sarah said, turning to John. "Thanks for the bouquet."

"What?" His eyebrows squinched into a frown.

"The flowers. They're beautiful."

"What flowers?" What flight of fantasy was she off on now?

"The ones you sent. An enormous, wonderful display."

"Must have been Pierre, your fan from the stage crew."

"No, I asked him. Besides, he couldn't afford such a gorgeous bouquet."

"Sare, I'm not in the mood for another mystery. I didn't send any flowers."

Sarah frowned. "You're sure?"

"For god's sake, of course, I'm sure!"

CHAPTER 12

The three of them — Ben cleaned up in fresh jeans and flip-flops — were back in the living room with its eclectic collection of Louis XV antiques and modern seating arrangement of low chairs around a large glass-topped coffee table, uncorked bottles of red and white within easy reach, cheese and fresh veggies, soft jazz mellow under the conversation.

"So, babe, you've got another admirer," John teased. "Someone sending you flowers. No card?"

"It just said 'Sarah' in block letters. That's all."

"Where are they?" John pushed. "Why didn't you bring them home?"

"It was a huge vase, almost an urn. Too heavy to carry. But I took a picture."

She headed for the kitchen and retrieved her backpack.

John looked at the photo then passed her cell phone to Ben. "Wow, huge is right." He raised his eyebrows at Sarah. "That's a very expensive arrangement. Fess up. You must have a rich admirer. As you said, unlikely it's someone who subsists on theater work. Or that techie from the Apple store? What's his name?"

"Regis. I haven't seen him lately."

"Ben, what are you staring at?" John reached over and took the phone from his partner. "Gee. That ink dripping off the card looks kind of like blood. Is that it?"

Ben didn't respond other than to shake his head.

"So, back to the possible admirers," John said. "What about that Dapper Dan you and Miranda picked up at the zoo?"

"Adeel? Don't be silly. He asked me out, but I'm too busy with rehearsals and Miranda."

Ben stopped a morsel of cheese mid-way to his mouth and picked up the phone again with a quizzical expression. "Something there is I know about *ça*."

"What do you mean? Familiar?" John asked.

"Don't know," Ben said, still staring at the phone.

"The flowers or the vase?" John asked. "That blob of blood-colored ink is certainly eye-catching."

"Don't know," Ben said again.

"A weird bouquet," John prodded. "The leaves look almost like hollyhock. Strange, kind of oriental vase. Why would it be familiar?"

"*Je ne sais pas*. But it itches my brain."

CHAPTER 13

Sarah was just settling onstage into Georgie's old chair, squirming, thinking about that puddle of blood — or whatever it was she'd seen the night of the murders — when the cops arrived again. Four of them, none in uniform, were led by the homicide detective, Jean Vidal, Mary's friend.

Were they never going to get this show in shape? These constant interruptions are brutal. Of course, the police had to find the murderer, or we'll never feel safe. But still, Sarah fretted that she'd soon be as old as her character if things didn't move along. I wasted time, and now doth time waste me. One had a job to do — and that was rehearse!

"Ah, Mademoiselle Sarah. *Ça va?*"

"I'm fine, thank you, Detective, but we were just beginning to rehearse. Surely a missing purse doesn't warrant more sleuthing." God, this guy is nice and trying to help. That sounded awfully sharp when he was just doing his job.

"Purse?"

"I think the French call them a *sac.*" From sharp to snippy, why couldn't she shut up?

"I'm familiar with the word. I didn't know you had lost such a one."

"Sorry. Since we've all answered so many questions, I assumed you must be after something new."

Can it, stupid! What is wrong with me? I'm obviously much more threatened by this new role than I'll admit, even to myself.

"I see," he said with a faint smile and an almost imperceptible bow from the waist. "Now we must justify our work, no?"

Sarah felt her face go hot. She must be crimson. "Forgive me. I'm being quite rude."

"So, tell me about your missing purse."

"Oh, it's not me, but the new woman doing our costumes. She told one of the crew earlier that she couldn't find her handbag or scissors. She claims a rip in a dress that Rachel wears on stage was cut, so it gave her this notion they were stolen."

"Ah, yes, Rachel. The actress who makes the other sister."

"Well, she plays her."

Rachel and the other actors, Margery, Sommes, and Paul, who was the waiter, had left their places and gathered around.

"The seamstress seems to be suggesting there is a thief among us," Sarah said, "but I bet she'll find both the missing items when she gets home tonight."

"And the dress was torn?" Vidal frowned. "Interesting."

"Cut," Sarah said. "Cut." She smiled at Vidal. "Not the unkindest of all. Rachel's still alive."

Vidal's eyes flickered. His jaw tightened. Nothing more.

Sarah put her hand to her forehead, closed her eyes, and said to herself, bite your damn tongue.

"So," Sommes intervened, "could you give us some sort of idea what progress the Paris police have made to solve these grisly murders?"

"We like to check things here more. Yes, it is mystery how

a stranger enters the stage, but no person sees it is not the proper actress, herself who is already murdered downstairs."

Sarah gasped. "You're sure that wasn't Georgie that I saw leaving?"

"Quite," Vidal pronounced as though he'd learned his English in a British finishing school. "Even Madame Rachel, who sat right beside, could not tell."

"A mystery, indeed," sniffed Sommes.

"And you also, sir, claim to have seen nothing," Vidal countered.

"If you'd bother to check, Detective, it's right in the lines of the play. Sarah, who plays my wife — or did — says, 'Don't look now, but those old ladies are staring at us.'"

"My vision was blurry." Rachel's tone was defensive. "I caught a strange odor and looked over to my left."

"We think it's possible," Sommes said, "that someone sprayed something near her."

"Whoever it was had to know the play," Paul said.

"And the setup of the stage," Rachel added.

"*Exactement,*" said Vidal. "We surmise the killer limp off with use of a cane. The lights man must have seen the interloper, made to intervene, been beaten by the cane and then garroted with it by the ropes, making lights to go out."

"And the knife," said Sarah. "It looked like our stage prop. The killer knew that, too, Detective. What do you know about that?"

"And now, you say the dress Madame Rachel wore has been torn. I will speak to the costume lady."

"Cut," Sarah said. "Cut."

CHAPTER 14

Sarah dawdled around the set after the rehearsal, hanging back eyeing the rear door until she saw that all the other actors had left. Then she headed down the circular stairs.

She skirted the offensive dressing table with its glaring bright bulbs where Georgie had bled to death and moved to a dark corner of the basement dressing room. She opened and began rummaging around in the old trunk she kept there, looking for the sexy new pair of silver kid, sling-back pumps she'd bought last week at Bon Marché. Way too much to spend in any case, but with her precarious job situation it was ridiculous. Still, she hadn't been able to resist — the terror of two murders and the stress of careening after a four-year-old had played havoc with her brain. Now she seemed to have lost the what-should-have-been diamond-encrusted shoes! Ah hell, do not mourn a mischief that is past and gone. "I must move on."

"*Comment*?" came back at her from behind a folding screen. Damn! Once again blurting out thoughts, sure she was alone down here — didn't want her fellow players to see those absurdly expensive shoes. What had possessed her to leave them here, probably with the price tag still on!

"It's only me," she called out. "Sarah."

The first thing she saw was a long, thin, gleaming pair of very sharp scissors. Very sharp indeed, ending in a needle-like point. Carrying them, thrust ahead of her like a spear, was Ann-Sophie, the seamstress who'd signed on with the company to make costume adjustments after cast members were switched around. The very same woman who'd told police that not only had her handbag been stolen, but her scissors as well.

"So," Sarah said, "did you find your purse, too?"

"*Comment*?" Non-comprehension in the bright blue eyes behind stylish, gold-rimmed, granny glasses. Ah, yes, Sarah remembered, the trendy young woman purportedly spoke no English, although most all other thirty-something Parisians who she'd encountered had at least a smattering. Sarah found something distinctly suspicious in that, especially since Ann-Sophie got on her bad side this afternoon by implying that someone in the cast was a thief.

"Well, now, Mistress No-English," Sarah spat out, "I don't suppose you've seen a new pair of silver shoes." She looked down at the svelte French woman's feet. "Just about your size, I'd judge."

"*Comment*?"

Sarah glared at her and was moving past, heading for the spiral stairs, when a bunch of flowers caught her eye. More of the same? Another bouquet. A thinner vase this time, but still earthen with jug handles and mosaic-like hand-painting on its base. Not fulsome flowers like the others, just perhaps a dozen long stems with some unidentifiable red blooms. She looked for a message, but there was none. Only a plastic cord that might have carried a card but was cleanly severed. Appeared to have been cut. Perhaps by scissors?

"A gift to you?" Sarah asked Ann-Sophie, gesturing toward the flowers.

"Comment?"

Sarah pulled her phone from her bag and took a picture. We'll see what Ben has to say about this! Was someone in the theater playing mind games?

Outside, Sarah felt like marching into a police station and demanding to know what was going on! A lot of good that would do. She knew the words for hello, goodbye, and how are you. The cops would say goodbye, or better yet, lock her up.

But murder was all around! Was Ann-Sophie being menacing with those scissors? And why would she lie that she'd lost them? Or did she simply find them after she claimed they were stolen?

I am in blood, stepp'd in so far that should I wade... Sarah shook herself. Macbeth was guilty, she wasn't! Besides, there had to be something she could do! What? Aye, that is the question.

Who could have first killed Blane Gowan then Georgie? And was Sarah next? For taking the part of the blind woman? Was it because of the role? Some disgruntled actress who felt she should have been cast? Someone with a grudge against Gomez? And who were these mysterious producers? CIA? Or whatever that Brit spy bunch was called?

As Gomez had explained, at the beginning the producer had made a last-minute substitution of Blane, a spy whose cover job was as an actress. She was supposed to catch the crooks who'd tampered with Miranda's suitcase but got thrown from a speeding train for her trouble. How ironic was that. A spy playing at being an actress. What a lark! But was it a role to kill for?

Who else would care enough about a tiny, sort of fringe, off-Broadway kind of production? Even if there were eventual plans to take it to both Broadway and the West End. Maybe the two murders weren't connected? Maybe Blane got killed for being a spy and Georgie was done-in by a disgruntled ex-husband? If that were the case, how would the police ever sort it out?

Sarah stiffened her resolve. She must change her focus, just as Mary had said, to who the killer was instead of when the cops would release the theater so they could rehearse! She yanked out her phone and called Mary, asking that they meet at John's as soon as Sarah could pick up Miranda at school.

"We need to start trying to sort this out. I fear we all are in danger again."

CHAPTER 15

Mary eyed her three friends as she sipped tea seated on a high stool at the big granite island in John's kitchen. Her entire apartment in her so-called changing Belleville neighborhood would fit in here with room to spare.

Ben, rousted from his studio, barefoot and in paint-spattered jeans. Sarah and John, the old college pals, heads together studying her cell phone, a symbiotic pair. The three had coffee and were munching from a bowl of freshly showered, plump green grapes.

Miranda and Bisquit were happily playing some form of doggie tag, running in and out through the dining room and double salon that strung across the front of the apartment.

Sarah passed her phone with the new photo over to Ben. "See what you think."

"What's all this about?" asked Mary, reaching for a quick look before handing it back. "I seem to have arrived in the middle of this movie."

"Someone keeps leaving Sarah flowers," John said.

"The last batch had no tag," Sarah said. "Cut off even in the blossoms of my sin."

Mary just closed her eyes and shook her head. Trying to

ever make sense of what this one was saying, or doing, for that matter, went beyond reason.

John grinned. "No signature on the first card, but addressed to Sarah in dripping red ink. On the second, the card had been severed. Sarah suspected the new seamstress. Both bouquets were left in the dressing room, and were in similar vases."

Ben suddenly jumped off his stool, waving Sarah's cell. "I think I have answer to this puzzle. *Un pompier* by name of Georges Rochegrosse. I'll look." He strode down the long hall that led to bedrooms and his studio.

"What?" John all but screeched. "A fireman?"

Mary laughed. "Since my Paul was a painter, I can answer that. It's a rather pejorative term for an artist who is not well thought of, who doesn't quite make the grade."

"That's crazy," John said. "We're talking about vases of flowers."

Ben was back, his finger holding his place in a thick art tome. He dropped it with a flourish onto the granite counter. "*Voila*." He flipped the book open to an array of biblical scenes, many dark and foreboding. Bloody battles. Women shackled, women nude, women being killed.

"So, where are the flowers?" John still sounded more than skeptical.

"Observe *ça*." Ben flipped to a different page. "And *ça*."

"You're right!" said John. "Each is pretty close to the bouquets Sarah got. And this one, with the tall red stems, has a nude woman looking at herself in a mirror."

G. Rochegrosse

"There was a Rochegrosse, how you say, *rétrospectif, en revue* in Moulins, some years before. They call it *Les Fastes de la Decadence.*"

"Wow," said Mary, "*The Splendor of Decadence.*"

"*Exactement*," replied Ben, wearing a very self-satisfied look.

"You mean this guy is menacing me?" Sarah demanded. "Oh, fine villain."

"*Non.* He is *mort.* Many years."

"Are you sure?"

"Of course," Ben was emphatic. "It says here. Buried in Montparnasse cemetery — it is…"

"I know exactly where it is," Sarah said. "Miranda and I have been there."

Hearing her name, Miranda skidded up, Bisquit yapping at her heels. She reached with sticky fingers toward the book. "Pictures."

Ben slapped her hand. "*Touche pas.*"

Sarah leaped up. "Ben, you can't do that."

Miranda ran to Sarah, and Bisquit started barking.

John was up, out of his chair. "For god's sake, everyone. We're getting off track here. Sit, calm down. Let's have a glass of wine."

"I'll have apple juice," Miranda said. "Mommy doesn't let me drink wine yet."

The adults burst out laughing. Sarah hugged Miranda, bending to ruffle her curls from her perch on the barstool.

Ben hurried to pass out wine glasses. John put out a slab of cheese then poured.

"Okay," said John, "let's get back to business. Now tell me, please, Miss Sarah, just what were you and Miranda doing at Montparnasse Cemetery?"

"Looking for Bernhardt's grave, but we found Baudelaire instead."

"Oh," moaned Mary. "I thought we were trying to solve a murder here. Instead, we're going to digress into *Flowers of Evil*"?

Ben laughed, slapping his hand hard on his book. "*Exactement.* This *pompier* here *dessiné* the cover for an edition of the *poème.*"

"That's the word the crazy man at the grave used," Sarah said.

"No," said Miranda. "He said *poésie*. Poetry."

"Let's move along," said Mary. "What's the issue? What happened? You went to look for Bernhardt's grave at Montparnasse when it's at Père Lachaise. Then what?"

"Everyone's always blaming me," snapped Sarah. "Well, this wasn't my fault. That's where the librarian sent me — gave me the map locator, the site number. But she got the two Bs mixed up."

"Some librarian," said Mary. "I think you should work a bit more on your French."

"Okay, okay," John injected. "What did the librarian say?"

"There, everything is order and beauty, richness, quiet and pleasure."

Mary burst out laughing. "That's Baudelaire, all right. She sent you, with his very own words, straight to his memorial in Montparnasse."

"What do you mean?" Sarah demanded.

"Sweet babe, you…" Mary was still sputtering and found it hard to get the words out past her laughter. She looked around, and everyone at the table was glaring at her, Miranda had backed away from Sarah and was standing like a soldier, hands on hips, staring up at Mary. Even Bisquit was growling. Incredible how this scatterbrained showgirl had them all bedazzled.

Mary closed her eyes for a moment then started over. "I suspect the woman was trying to hit on you for a date. John, have you got an English copy of *Flowers of Evil*? I'll show you the poem."

If nothing else, she knew her French literature. That's what she'd come here from Ireland to study before marrying Paul, and then widowed. She might be teaching English to French students who couldn't care less. But, damn it, she knew her Baudelaire.

Until John found the book, the others sat in silence, drinking. Except Miranda, who lost interest in the games adults play and resumed her doggie-tag romp with Bisquit.

The book in hand, Mary said, "It's called 'An Invitation to Voyage.'"

"Oh my god," said Sarah, her face slowly taking on the shade of the rosé she was drinking.

Mary read, "'My child, my sister, think of the delight of going far off and living together! Of loving peacefully, loving and dying in the land that bears your resemblance!'"

The room went silent except for the kid and the clattering dog.

Mary cleared her throat. "I'll skip a bit, but here's your phrase. 'There, everything is order and beauty, richness, quiet and pleasure.'"

"But, cripes," said John. "How can you assume it's a lesbian thing? Doesn't he speak of dying there? Read it again. Can't the there refer back to death?"

"I am undone." Sarah burst into tears.

CHAPTER 16

The doorbell rang, and Miranda was off and running down the long hall, her golden retriever, Chess, barreling behind, before Sarah could hoist herself from the floor where she and her niece had been playing Calabash.

The door was slammed shut by the time Sarah reached her. Miranda flashed past, dancing, package in hand, along the book-and-toy-lined shelves, heading for the living room. "It's a present. It's for me."

"Hold on, little kiddo. Let me look."

"No. It's from Daddy. He always sends me presents when he's gone."

Sarah grabbed for the package, but her niece was quicker, gleefully shouting, "It's mine."

Miranda ran across the room and slapped her booty on the seat of a straight-back chair in order to operate at eye level.

"Look," she pointed at the brown paper parcel with no postage. "I think that says Miranda."

"No, babe, only the address." That was clear even from a distance.

Sarah skidded up, but too late. Miranda was already

ripping at the wrapping. "Be careful." She was trying not to screech. "We don't know what's inside."

"It's red," Miranda said. "I love red!" She snatched off the rest of the paper and held up the rubberized fabric as it unfolded. "A raincoat. It's a raincoat. Daddy sent me."

Sarah's eyes widened. "Oh my god, it's a mackintosh. A red mackintosh!" The film image of a dead child dressed in blood-red floating, Ophelia-like, in *Don't Look Now* swam before her eyes. It must be some kind of diabolical threat! She tried to snatch it from her niece but was stunned to find how strong the kid was when it came to a tug of war.

"Miranda, don't touch it. We've got to call the police, your mother." She knocked the wrapping from the chair with a toe, guiding it under the couch. She'd seen enough police TV shows to know about smudging fingerprints.

Miranda already had the vile thing on and was prancing around. It fit perfectly, as though it were made to measure! A tiny, attached hood hung down the child's back. Sarah could barely control her trembling fingers as she punched in her sister's number, telling her to come home. She then called John.

"It's the color of blood," she whispered, not wanting Miranda to make the association. "It can't be the crazy librarian. It's got to be someone in the show." But she realized, as soon as she'd said it, that wasn't logical. Anyone could have seen that scary psychological thriller set in the streets of Venice.

What to do while they waited for the others to arrive? Miranda couldn't be stopped. As though she were possessed. What potion had she drunk? She ran from room to room, looking and posing mirror to mirror. Sarah was trying to damp-down her own hysteria. Once the package was opened, the genie was out of the bottle. More important to not frighten Miranda than snatch the thing off. But her niece looked so much like the film child in her red rain gear it was all Sarah could do to keep from screaming and ripping at the hideous thing. She mustn't. She had to protect Miranda from knowing this was some sort of awful menace.

Who could be so cruel? Was the killer sending a threat through the child? Must be. No other explanation. The mackintosh never appears in the play, but it was the striking visual that everyone always remembers from the film. It was the red that Sarah saw on Georgie's chair when she'd disappeared from the stage. No, Georgie wasn't there! Vidal had told them this very morning that she was already dead. Stabbed to death in the basement. Just what had Sarah seen? The confusion of that night haunted her dreams.

Vidal and two colleagues were the first to arrive. When the bell rang, Miranda and Chess swooped off to open the door. Sarah was close enough behind to see the stricken look on the detective's face when he saw the child in the red slicker. No wonder Mary was taken with the man. His look of horror overlaid with tenderness was endearing.

"*Bonjour, Petit Chaperon Rouge,*" he bent to pat Miranda's arm. "You are quite the detective still, I see. You have found another clue in our mystery."

Red Riding Hood swelled almost to bursting at the mention of her sleuthing abilities.

"Invite the policemen in, Miranda," Sarah said, backing away as the child opened the door wide to make room for the two men and a tiny, smartly dressed young woman.

"Is it really a clue?" Miranda asked.

"*Bien sûr*," Vidal replied. "And now we must inspect, *s'il te plait*," putting his hand out. The woman donned latex gloves and produced a plastic bag.

Miranda obediently took off the slicker,

"*Etes-vous une détective*?" Miranda's voice was filled with wonder as she handed over the shiny red thing.

"*Oui*," the tiny woman replied. Even in her *talons*, as the French called them, she was still not too much taller than the child. "But I speak English. I studied in Minneapolis."

"Oh," Miranda said. "I don't know what that is. I'm a detective, too. Not so grown up yet, but I can find clues. I'm four and a half and three quarters."

"Well," Sarah said, moving her eyes over the luminous cream of the petite cop's silk blouse worn with a business-like but finely cut suit. "We have a crime to solve. Time and the hour runs through the roughest day."

Sarah smiled faintly at the woman's puzzled look. Hmp, her English isn't as good as she thinks, if she stumbles over Shakespeare.

As they moved along the hall, the bell sounded again. Miranda and Chess scrambled back to the door as Sarah led the police into the living room.

"Hi, Uncle John." Miranda's voice rang down the hall. "There's a lady detective, just like me."

"What's this about a red mackintosh?" John stood, surveying the scene from the living room doorway, a worried frown stretching his face. Vidal was bent down, gloves on, to extricate the brown wrapping where Sarah had toed it under the couch.

"Vicki should be here shortly," John announced. "Mary too."

Vidal looked up, and Sarah thought she saw a glint in his eye at that last bit of news, but he said, "We must to have our investigation finished before this is to become a family gathering."

He lifted himself up and smiled at Miranda. "Now, Miss *Petit Chaperon Rouge*, we must talk. You received the package, non? And who, *s'il te plait*, delivered it?"

"Nobody," Miranda said. "It was just there when Chess and I opened the door."

"The dog," Sarah offered at Vidal's quizzical look.

"I see. No one there. So, one of my detectives must speak *immédiatement* to the concierge. Georges," he gestured at the third detective, "*allez*," then turned back to Miranda. "Nothing? Just the package?"

Miranda nodded. "It's a clue. I'm good at finding clues."

"*Bien sûr.* We have many paths to follow while you and your aunt search for Madame Bernhardt." He looked up at Sarah. "There is Monsieur Adeel at Jardin des Plantes. The librarian with the lipstick black. The seamstress with scissors. And the man with the tie of plastic at the cemetery. Is anyone missed?"

"Well, there was the morgue. We met Georgie's family and her ex-husband. He might be a bit like Bernhardt's Jacques."

"Jacques? I fear I am not a scholar of the great actress."

"The husband she always loved and tried to support in his acting career, sometimes to the detriment of her own. Drugs, it's said."

"Ah," said Vidal, his eyes lighting up. "Husband, *c'est possible.*"

"I can't say." Miranda mimicked a very grown-up sound with her imperious tone. "I wasn't at the morgue. I was in school."

"A good place for you, my little Miss," Vidal said. "It might be good if you would leave off detective work for a while."

Sarah was surprised. It was the first time she'd heard Vidal be short with anyone. He no doubt was right. But she hadn't taken Miranda to the morgue. And who knew they would be running into suspects at the zoo. She'd felt guilty all along about taking her to the cemetery. Yet it turns out that Parisians treated their burial grounds like historical monuments. It was surely complicated here. Sometimes she wished she were back in Anaheim, but not often. "I don't quite understand why everyone we meet is a suspect," she said.

Vidal frowned. "With murder, we must check all things. You received strange flowers. You have lost your silver shoes. One would guess that now you'll be searching the proper grave of Madame Bernhardt. We would prefer that you stay home with Mademoiselle Miranda. Yet nothing for us to do but follow your encounters."

John spoke up for the first time. "You're right, Detective. We'd all like for them to stay home. But one is more incorrigible than the other."

At that, Chess began barking and skidded down the hall to the front door, Miranda close behind.

"Oh, woe," Sarah said. "Vicki's home. Now I'm really in for it."

Chaos reigned for a brief interlude while Vicki berated Sarah, Mary arrived, and John made coffee. Then all settled down for a serious discussion of just what was going on.

"Of course her father didn't send Miranda a red, rubberized raincoat from Cairo," Vicki spat out. "I don't need to phone Bill to verify that. But I certainly plan to speak to him shortly. He needs to be home more, not constantly off chasing wars and earthquakes around the world. And, with all this nuttiness going on, I obviously need to find a new babysitter."

"NO!" Miranda and Sarah shouted in unison.

"This is not my fault," Sarah said.

"You're the one in that damn play."

"Good lord, you can't blame her for that," John said.

"The play is the center of the problems," Vicki countered. "There have been two mur… Miranda, babe, let's go to your room and find you something to play with."

"No. I'm the one who found the clue. I can stay." Miranda turned to the policewoman for support. "I can help," she said, reaching out for the petite cop's hand in a clear plea.

A deep frown crossed Sarah's face. "Well, I'm the babysitter. I'll go to her room with her, and we'll play a game."

"No!" Miranda stomped her foot. "I'm a detective too."

Sarah looked around the room and took a deep breath. She didn't need to hear all this palaver. John could fill her in later. No doubt, it would be about how Sarah was scatterbrained and actors irresponsible.

"Look," she said to Miranda, "the detectives are taking notes. We'll go do the same. Talk about what we saw at the zoo and what the guy said at Baudelaire's monument. Then we'll have some real evidence to compare. Come on, kiddo, that's how detectives work. We can't get anything done with everyone talking at once."

Miranda looked at her mother. Vicki nodded a yes. "Sounds fine. I guess your aunt has a good plan, for once."

CHAPTER 17

"We can mark things down," Miranda said, picking up a magic erasing slate after her bedroom door closed. "And I'll call the police lady and give her our clues."

Sarah bit her lip. Vicki was abandoning her for another babysitter, and Miranda had already switched allegiance. The smack of that thought made her eyes sting. "So, start writing," she snapped.

"Maybe you should do that," Miranda said, handing her the pad. "I only make block letters."

Sarah looked around at the familiar room with its faint scent of Disney spiced by international touches — a Moroccan watercolor, a Bavarian doll — and sucked in a sharp breath at the thought of what they'd been through in the past few weeks. Vicki said she wanted her daughter to ultimately be an American child, but with all this crime swirling around, the poor kid was hardly a child anymore.

Little more than two weeks ago, Vicki had fought off a thug who'd come through this very same balconied window to kidnap Miranda but managed only to make off with the kid's suitcase, thinking it contained a list of illicit art dealers.

"We don't need some short cop in high heels to help us be detectives," Sarah said sharply.

Miranda studied her aunt for a moment then replied carefully. "But you're an actress. I'm the detective."

Sarah's laugh was short and dry. "I suppose I'd have to go along with that, but I would hope you'd crime-solve with *me*. We're a team. Weren't we imprisoned in the van together when the crooks were trying to drive off with stolen art?"

"Yes." Miranda was still studying her aunt. She finally emitted a heavy sigh followed by a resigned look. "I suppose I need to practice before a real police officer will trust me."

Sarah grimaced. Why can't I get rid of the refrain, these words are razors? I wish I'd never played Lady Macbeth. My whole life has turned into a Scottish tragedy. "So," she said straightening against the hurt, "let's decide what we should do."

"We have a murder to solve," Miranda declared.

"That's what the police are for," Sarah growled. "I have a job to do. I've got to keep that play alive, or I won't *have* a job. Bernhardt inspires me. Maybe we could find her real grave tomorrow."

Miranda was insistent. "I'm the one who discovered the red raincoat."

"Fine," Sarah said stiffly. "What next?"

A sly kid smile. "We can go back to the zoo."

"And what clue will we unearth?"

"What's unearth?"

Sarah rolled her eyes. "What is it you want to do there?"

"Visit the skeleton museum."

"The what?"

"It's fun, like Halloween. It's a building at the zoo."

"Fine." Sarah stood up abruptly. "Tomorrow when I pick you up."

"And we can go for cakes and tell them we're looking for Adeel. The detective said he was a clue."

"Not a clue, Miranda. Just a person who might have sent me the flowers."

"What flowers?"

Sarah shook her head. Babysitting was a tough job. And having kids? Playing Lady Macbeth was a whole lot easier.

CHAPTER 18

Trying to clear her head, Sarah walked slowly to that night's rehearsal, blind to the sights and sounds of Paris around the theater.

She was still shaken by the delivery of the red mackintosh. Someone, she suspected, was out to get her for taking on this role. And a perfect way to threaten was through her niece. Was she jeopardizing Miranda's safety just for a challenging part? She didn't even want the damned thing. She simply wanted the play to proceed — and to pay homage to poor Georgie by keeping the role alive. Georgie had been thrilled at getting the part of the psychic.

What to do? Sarah thought back on her experience as Lady Macbeth last year in London. Only minor mishaps for that production, each probably blown out of proportion because of the endless myths surrounding The Scottish Play. She'd thought that had taught her to be immune to the constant sightings by cast members of so-called ominous signs, but here she was again trying to divine danger. In London, they'd actually gotten through the entire run with little more than an adult sprained ankle, a kiddie outbreak of runny noses among Macduff's children, and Sarah's purse being snatched on the

Underground at Charring Cross, followed by a break-in at her rental flat.

Sarah knew her theatrical history, and foul luck had dogged the show from its very first production in the 1600s when the boy playing Lady Macbeth died backstage. Death, destruction, and fatal stabbings continued to modern day. Shakespeare was alleged to have begun the trend of refusing to reference its title by referring to it in disgust as "that play" after King Edward I took a dislike to it. In 1672, the actor playing Macbeth killed the Duncan character on stage with a dagger that'd been substituted for a fake one.

Sarah couldn't shake the fear that the stabbing of Georgie with a knife that looked just like their stage prop harkened back to the production of The Scottish Play they'd been in together. Vicki and her friends laughed at Sarah's stretch from then to now and from Duncan to a blind psychic, but her theatrical bones understood these things. Over the years, sets had collapsed, theaters were burned, one in 1721 by a disgruntled audience member. But Sarah kept telling herself, the present show was NOT The Scottish Play. Why were these things happening? Her friends kept telling her she was too suggestible, too myth-oriented. But this was no myth. These killings were real. Was she next?

And the furies, the witches, the Weird Sisters. *Wyrd*, she remembered, in Shakespeare's script. Scholars and historians placed strange importance on their meaning with all sorts of interpretations from comic Scottish witches to the *parcae*, the fates of classical Roman mythology. Could there really be something to the curse of the play? King Edward's hatred was said to have been because the incantations were too realistic.

But again, she told herself, We are not doing Shakespeare, so why did she keep referencing The Scottish Play?

She kept seeing in her mind's eye the dead Georgie, face smashed down among the makeup jars, the blood, the broken glass. Georgie's body in repose, shadowed by the stained-glass window of the morgue. Her husband so languidly strolling off after the Weird Sisters, the Furies, had thrown him from the viewing room. He glided almost, just the way whoever had impersonated Georgie slid from the stage.

Oh my God! That husband of hers! He had been hired to play a witch, but he was fired so fast, Sarah barely remembered him, what he looked like. Detective Vidal was searching for clues, she certainly must remind him again about this one. Most of the cast wanted to believe it was the CIA, or MI6, or something. She was just going to have to settle it herself! Ben would help. He knew the name of the man who had painted flowers like those she'd received. What kind of clue was that? Did it mean the killer was an art historian? What nonsense was that? And Mary had said he was such a poor painter the French called him a fireman. Nonsense indeed!

Sarah climbed down the spiral stairs and before she touched the bottom rung spotted more flowers — two white fulsome blooms on a single stem lying on the dressing table. No vase. The bouquets had gotten smaller and smaller. What did this spiraling down mean? That the end was near?

CHAPTER 19

Sarah was leaning on her favorite railing waiting for Miranda to come out of school thinking about the two white blossoms on a single stem. She worried Ben would be locked away again in his do-not-disturb studio. She hadn't been able to ask him last night what he knew about those flowers!

But what was that artist's name, the one he derisively called a fireman? Ben had said his work wasn't thought highly of and that perhaps the Musée d'Orsay had only one or two. She'd see what she could find herself while she was waiting. Weird name, something with fat in it. She typed a few versions into Google then suddenly got a hit – Rochegrosse, that was it! Fireman, indeed. The guy was certainly prolific — tons and tons of pictures and information, but she needed a book. The American Library was the obvious place, but she couldn't bear the thought of having to face that leering Tiffany with her awful black lipstick.

What was the damned French word for book? *Livre*! And here was "Georges-Antoine Rochegrosse: *Les Fastes de la Décadence*." The very exhibit Ben had mentioned! How did people survive before Google? Hmm. Available at a store with the goofy name FNAC. How did you pronounce that? Gad, they seemed to have a million outlets in Paris. *Okay, Google map, find one near me.* Montparnasse sounded good — could probably walk. And here came the horde, Miranda waving a paper that appeared to be one of her crayon renderings.

"Oh, FNAC." Miranda, her usual imperious self. "I know the way. Daddy and I go there all the time. They have good video games."

Sarah was in no position to judge the accuracy of how often her niece visited, but she could attest to the fact that the kid didn't know the way. At the first big boulevard, Miranda dictated a left turn, in which direction Sarah could see the imposing gold dome of Napoleon's tomb, Les Invalides. And to the right, standing tall against the sky was the city's highest and most hated building that even greenhorn Sarah knew Parisians derisively called the black widow, or middle finger, or even worse. "That's the Montparnasse Tower, Miranda, can't miss it. So it's gotta be that way."

Miranda stopped, seeming to ponder the wisdom of her aunt's direction, almost literally dragging her feet.

"Come on, let's move it," Sarah snapped. "I've got an evening rehearsal and still have to take you home by time Mommy gets there."

"I know my way home."

Sarah looked at her pouting niece and reached over to ruffle the blonde curls. "I'm sure you do, sweet babe, but it's more fun together. Let's hurry. I've got a book to find."

Finally located, FNAC, with a nearly blot-out-the-sky view of the Ugly Tower straight down rue de Rennes, was absolutely huge and aswarm with seemingly crazed clientele. Up endless escalator levels, wow. An entire floor of nothing but books.

Miranda commanded the attention of a slightly balding, nondescript guy with FNAC on the back of his yellow and green fluorescent traffic-cop-type vest. A T-shirt under it proclaimed "Safe Swimming" in English. "I'll explain about the fireman," she told Sarah and immediately rattled off something in French to the bemused but not comprehending salesman.

"Here's the name," Sarah said, quickly writing out the letters Rochegrosse on the back of an old envelope, the first scrap she could rummage from her purse.

Mr. Safe Swim consulted his computer, produced a copy of *Les Fastes de la Décadence,* and explained something in French to Miranda as he handed the book over to Sarah. The artwork on the cover gave her chills.

"We have to pay on the ground floor," Miranda said. "It's called the *rez-de-chaussée*, NOT the first floor."

"Yes. You've explained that before."

She stared at the book's cover. No flowers, what was so unsettling? It seemed innocent enough. A beautiful woman in a long see-through veil, playing a lyre against the backdrop of an Arabic-looking mosaic wall, two long serpents, tongues flashing, stood at attention, and animals, perhaps horses, grazed below. A jewel around the pointed crown of the lady's hat, a tight choker adorning her neck. It was sumptuous but somehow took Sarah's breath away. Why "Decadence?" Was that just a synonym for opulence? Perhaps that's what the word actually means in French.

Georges-Antoine
Rochegrosse
LES FASTES DE LA DÉCADENCE
mab

"Look," squealed Miranda, "a detective book for kids." She excitedly grabbed from a large display what appeared to be a hard-cover comic book with, strangely, I.R.S. in its title. A man squatted down, holding his head in one hand and a revolver in the other.

"Why would a French kid's book be about the IRS?" Sarah asked. "Surely, it must mean something else in French."

"It's a detective book with pictures. I want it." Miranda was adamant.

"Now listen, little kiddo …"

"No. I want it."

Down the several escalators, the long lines of the checkout lanes looked like a giant supermarket. "Damn, I'm going to be late for rehearsal," Sarah grumbled.

As she shifted from one foot to the other, clutched Miranda's hand in the swirling crowd, she nonetheless tried to thumb through the heavy book. More than two hundred glossy pages, loaded with pictures, it was quite something. But it should be, at more than Thirty Dollars!

"If we're going to be detectives, we have to find more clues," Miranda said, squirming, unsuccessfully trying to worm out of Sarah's tight grasp. It was clear the kid wanted to escape to explore the tech-packed environment. What a disaster that would be. It could take hours to find her in this mob.

"My detective work is done for the day," Sarah snapped.

"You said we could go to the skeleton museum," Miranda whined.

"That's for another day. I've got to get to… Oh my god," Sarah gasped, dropping the book in her agitation. Nothing, at this point, not even murder, could cause her to let go of the precious cargo grasped in her other hand.

"What? What?" Miranda blanched. "Is someone going to shoot us?"

"No, no! I didn't mean to frighten you." Sarah bent to pick up the fallen tome, still clutching her niece's hand.

"But, look," she said, pointing at a glossy page with a shaking finger. "Two white flowers on a single stem, and that's Sarah Bernhardt holding it."

CHAPTER 20

Sarah tapped her cane, moving across the stage as the blind woman, and glanced out at the nearly empty auditorium through her dark glasses. Miranda was sitting quietly, the I.R.S. detective book in her lap, Gomez a row behind shouting out stage directions. Oh, the trials of looking after a child — Vicki had a news crisis and couldn't leave the office. They were going to have to find an auxiliary babysitter.

She had just started to deliver the all-powerful line "You saw us on the Vaporetto…" when the dark glasses quit working, she stumbled, she couldn't see, Rachel screamed, what was going on? Miranda's voice in a yelp of joy from her front row seat. Sommes hissed, "Take off your glasses. The lights are out."

Sarah yanked off the offending spectacles just as the thud of something crashing shuddered the floor beneath her feet to a symphony of breaking glass.

Which way to turn? Pitch dark, couldn't yet adjust her eyes, afraid to take a step. Miranda. She must find Miranda! Shards in every direction. This was what it was like to really be blind! She could identify the frightened voices of her colleagues but could make no sense of what was said. Were they speaking or just moaning, babbling incoherently? But nothing from Miranda since that last shout of happiness. What did that mean?

Just as suddenly, the lights blinked back on.

Sarah frantically scanned out as she started down the few auditorium steps then stopped, mid-step, in horror. Miranda was wearing the red mackintosh!

"Where did that vile thing come from? Take it off," Sarah screamed as she reached the child, yanking at the slicker. "You can't. It's horrible, dangerous." Terror clutched at her. She couldn't catch her breath.

"No, it's mine. Daddy sent it." Miranda twisted away and began kicking at her. Sarah tried to grab her, constrain her, but the child fought back as though possessed.

Gomez shot past, up the steps. "Is sabotage. The set is garbage."

Still clutching at Miranda, Sarah looked up. A huge light board lay strung across the stage, the back bistro table crushed, chairs scattered, shards of colored glass coated everything. Sarah's heart turned over. "Is everyone all right?" she called out.

Rachel stood center stage, tears running down her face. "A miracle," she replied.

"Call police," Gomez shouted.

"Ask for Detective Vidal," Sarah hollered back. He could bring some sanity to this. Miranda, struggling against her, seemed crazed.

Sommes bounded down to join Sarah's battle to contain Miranda. "What?" he exclaimed. "A red slicker! Holy Christ, like the film."

"Child, hand it over," he tried in a soothing, sympathetic

voice Sarah had never heard before. The guy's human, she thought.

"It's mine," the kid said defiantly, wrenching free of Sarah and vaulting over the back of a theater seat, out of Sarah's reach. "The police took it away. Now they gave it back."

"Gave it back?" Sarah wheezed, trying to keep up with Miranda as she bounded from seat to seat. "That's insane."

"It must be a clue in this frightful incident," Sommes said, holding out his hand to the kicking kid — shrouded in the red slicker, hood up — trying to reason with her.

Sarah abruptly stopped the useless chase, felt her world crumbling. My niece has gone mad, whose horrid image doth unfix my hair. The Scottish Play had come back to haunt her. She was convinced that Georgie had died because of her role in it, but the drawn-out wrath — the sinister flowers – was being saved for Sarah, who had played the murderous Lady Macbeth. She could never forgive herself for insisting that this new, jinxed play be kept going. Her colleagues must hate her, assembled on stage, cast and crew, watching in frightened confusion. But this was her responsibility! She straightened her shoulders and again joined Sommes trying to corral Miranda.

As they moved on her from each end, Miranda clambered over the back of a seat and scooted down a new row. Sommes stepped over to block her path up the aisle. Sarah, not so agile as Miranda, had to go to the end of her row to circle round to help Sommes pen in the kid. Each row that they entered, Miranda vaulted another seat back, and the row-by-row chase proceeded up toward the back of the theater.

"Vat is happening? Vat is going on?" Gomez was yelling from the stage. "Where are police? Show is kaput."

As the director shouted, Sarah looked his way. Where is the lovely Ann-Sophie of the sharpened scissors? She had thought all crew were on stage watching, but the seamstress was noticeably absent.

Making another futile grab at Miranda, Sarah spotted Vidal coming into the theater. She'd never been so happy to see the inquisitor. Maybe *he* could do something with this kid.

"So, Little Miss *Chaperon Rouge. Qu'est-ce que c'est?* You have found another clue?"

"It's mine."

"And where, *s'il tu plait*, did you obtain it?"

"Daddy sent it. They gave it to me."

"Who is they?"

"I don't know. Someone. The police took it away for a while, now they gave it back."

"Alas, I fear we must again take it," Vidal said, holding out his hand.

Miranda shook her head. "I'll give it to the lady detective."

"Sorry, Red Riding Hood, it's her day off," the cop replied.

CHAPTER 21

Sarah, along with her colleagues, watched from front row seats as uniformed police and a forensics team took over the stage inspecting the fallen light board. Vidal and another plain-clothes officer took the cast aside one by one for questioning.

Miranda, paying rapt attention, sat beside her aunt. "It's just like a TV show," she burbled.

Sarah, still stung by the kid's having asked for the short detective in high heels, didn't bother to reply. Sharper than a serpent's tooth. Yes, most certainly, they needed an auxiliary babysitter, probably a new one altogether! Why not? She ran herself all over Paris trotting this kid around, being late for rehearsals, missing readings, now fetching her here at the last minute for this mess, and what thanks does she get?

"I'll give it to the lady detective!" The wretched thanklessness! A serpent's tooth, indeed.

While Sarah pondered her own lot, Gomez roamed the aisle, exclaiming, "Is disaster. Vot to do?" periodically trying to mount the stage stairs only to be met by a police rebuff.

Vidal finally made his way over to Sarah, pulled her aside from Miranda and the others, and began in a low voice, almost a whisper. "Our worst fears have been realized, Mademoiselle. The cables to render support were severed."

Sarah drew a quick breath. "But no surprise."

"I also desire you to know that we did not allow the first red coat to leave from our property room – this one is new one and carries still more menace."

Vidal then echoed Rachel's earlier sentiment that it was a miracle that no one had been wounded or killed. "It is my considered judgment that the show must not to proceed. It would appear to be much too *dangereux*."

Sarah felt flat and empty. This entire experience had been debilitating, exhausting. Again, it flickered through her sluggish brain that she should point out to Vidal that the seamstress with the scissors didn't seem to be around. She also must tell him about the latest chilling flowers.

"And, *s'il vous plait*," he continued, in what was close to a plea as he prepared to move on to another cast member, "would be possible for you to aid in an *explication à Monsieur le directeur*."

This last brought a tiny half-smile to her lips. Little does he know that I'm probably the one who cares the most about keeping the play going because I'm worried I'll be thrown out of the country. Should I ask him if I'll lose my visa, or if my babysitting job will be enough to allow me to stay? Well, damn, maybe the lady detective can take over for me.

Finally, with Miranda at rapt attention quiet in her seat next to Sarah watching the forensics officers at work, Vidal took a position in front of the cast, his rumpled linen jacket bulging on the left with what was no doubt a gun. He leaned back on an elbow resting on the stage's edge, crossed one loafer-clad foot in front of the other, and informed them in his stilted English, speckled with French, that a preliminary search had turned up nothing other than a bit of flimsy cord that police surmised was used to temporarily hold the lights in place after the cables were cut. Thus the timing of the terrifying plunge had seemingly been left to chance.

Why would that be? Sarah wondered. A war of nerves? A way to keep playing with the entire cast, or just with her? As far as she knew, she was the only one receiving the mysterious flowers. Surely the others would have mentioned it, if they were. And the Bernhardt picture with the exact same white spider mums seemed to confirm she was the one the killer was after.

The flowers could wait, Sarah decided, too complicated to explain. Now was the time to bring up Georgie's ex. Vidal and all of them knew, of course, that he had been at the viewing, but she hadn't remembered then about his very brief connection with the London production of The Scottish Play.

"Inspector," she said, in a voice loud enough to benefit them all, "Georgie's ex-husband, who we know is now in Paris, has some working knowledge of the theater. He was fired after a few hours from a show she and I both were in."

The hubbub was instant, Sommes being the most vocal. "Why, pray tell, did you not inform us of this sooner?"

"I'd forgotten. I never even met the man. As I said, he was gone from the show within hours. Drugs, perhaps."

"I will check. Thank you." Vidal straightened from his slouch against the stage, cutting off the discussion.

Sarah then asked her recurring question: "Has anyone seen Ann-Sophie?"

CHAPTER 22

The cast and crew decided to reassemble at Gomez's rental to discuss their future after the police said they were again going to seal off the theater so they could continue their forensic work.

On the walk over, Sommes had the presence of mind to stop in a Nicolas package store for several bottles of wine. Always in character, Miranda, when they reached the lobby, rushed to the elevator and elbowed Gomez out of the way to push the call button.

This kid is truly annoying, Sarah decided, the detective in the talons can have her. Maybe New York! There's plenty of stage work there.

Upstairs, wine glasses in hand, Miranda safely ensconced in another room with juice, Sarah's cell phone and the kid detective book, the adults were stunned to hear Sommes insist they should keep the play going regardless of what the police advised.

"Theater jobs are hard to come by. This is a good-paying gig, we're in Paris, why not?"

"The why not is we might all be killed," Margery, ever the ingénue, uncharacteristically snapped.

Sarah's mouth literally flew open. Two countries heard from, and both totally unexpected. The first time the mousey one has expressed an opinion about anything, and no guts, no-glory Sommes! I can't believe it. He must be trying to escape alimony payments in England. Even worse, horrible thought, he could be the killer and wanting to knock us off, one by one. Or maybe only me, I'm the one getting the flowers. But why? He's snippy with me, but so what? And he was swell helping try to corral Miranda. A side of him she'd never seen before.

First reactions were amusing. Rachel responded to the unexpected Sommes as her usual contained self with nothing more than an "Oh my." Gomez emitted a thunderous, "Wunderbar." And Paul, the waiter, delivered an "I say!" The French crew wore a universal, not-sure-if-I'm-comprehending frown, accompanied by one or two *"Qu'est-ce que c'est?"*

The clatter of ensuing arguments was ear-splitting. Everyone talking and shouting at once. Enough to bring Miranda running in from her hideaway, eyes wide.

"I won't put my head on the block," Margery yelled.

"Your lifeless performances won't be missed," Sommes hissed, back to snippy self.

Pierre moved over to Sarah. "So *les Anglais*, not so stuffy, *non*?"

"A good job, *pourquoi pas*," shrugged the newly hired light tech.

"Because *le mec* before you is hanged by the neck," snapped the prop guy.

"Paris suits me," Paul chimed in. "Decidedly better weather than London."

Gomez stood up in the middle of the room and excitedly clapped his hands. "Is decided. The show must go on!"

"Can the police stop us?" Sarah asked.

"On what grounds?" Sommes snapped.

"Public safety, perhaps?" Sarah replied. "Detective Vidal said he considered it dangerous."

"Who to do *le rôle* Margery does?" Pierre asked.

Gomez shrugged. "Sarah is better for the wife, anyway."

"Fine," Rachel replied drily. "So, without Sarah filling in for the psychic, I'm to play both sisters? First, I'll say one's lines, then get up from the table, go to the other side, and say the other's?"

The prop man laughed. "Is *un problème.*"

"Yes," Rachel said. "You know very well, Mr. Gomez, that you scoured London agents before for the role of the psychic and got no takers. Two actresses already murdered. It's a death sentence."

Miranda moved over, hands on hips, to stand in front of Sarah. "So, is there a show?"

"I think we need more wine," Sommes said.

CHAPTER 23

Sarah's phone rang. It had grown dark, the cast still drinking and arguing about the pros and cons of keeping *Don't Look Now* alive.

It was Vicki. "Where the hell is Miranda? I'm getting calls here at work wanting to know where you are."

"Who's asking?"

"What difference does it make? Where are you?"

"Gomez's."

"Is Miranda okay? The police are looking for you."

"Are you sure? We just left them a couple of hours ago."

Vidal, it turned out, had contacted Vicki asking that the troupe return to the theater immediately. He had assumed that Miranda's mother would know better than anyone where to reach them.

"What's it about?" Sarah demanded. "We're sick of police."

"Get on over there and see what they want. Then take Miranda home. It's past her bedtime." Vicki hung up.

The rest of the troupe had all the same questions Sarah had, also her reluctance. Miranda was the only dissenter. "Let's go now. The police are fun."

When the eleven of them arrived, straggling along in

bunches, they were greeted by the ubiquitous yellow tape and armed guards. "Detective Vidal asked for us," Sarah explained. It took three different cops trying to sort out her English, even the words "Detective Vidal," before Miranda finally stepped in.

"How many ways can you say 'detective?'" Sarah grumbled, only to be told by the imperious child, "It's dE-teck-tEEfe."

Once Vidal was located, he solemnly led them into the theater, sat them down, and said, "Ann-Sophie is murdered."

Into the chorus of stunned whats? whys? and hows?, Miranda's voice rang out, "Who's Ann-Sophie?"

Amid the chaos of questions and off-putting answers from Vidal, Sarah's soul deflated into self doubt. This child is being warped by my surroundings. I must get her away from this horror. She truly needs a better babysitter. Poor Vicki is trying to be a supportive sister, but look at the price she's paying! No wonder she's cranky with me all the time. She's risking her child's serenity letting her participate in the chaos of my life.

Sarah worked to steady her voice. "She did sewing for the cast, Miranda, but this isn't something for us to worry about. Perhaps the detective will let us go now and get some ice cream." Her eyes pleaded with Vidal.

"*Bien sûr*," he replied with a knowing nod. "There is perhaps a café just down the street."

"No! I want to hear about the murder." Miranda was adamant.

A murmur of support rose up from those seated around. As they shifted, stirred in their seats, Sarah sensed a collective warmth. It was a first. In her several weeks here, she'd never felt they were a troupe. Suddenly it was a single unit, all with the same goal.

"Surely," Rachel said quietly, "we would benefit from being interviewed individually."

"Quite," said Sommes.

"And is better for some," said the prop man, "if spoken in French to each."

Miranda brightened. "I'll give my clues to the lady detective."

Sarah winced. She was out of the picture, whether she wanted to be or not.

Vidal smiled in relief. "So, Detective du Bois will speak with *la petite mademoiselle* tomorrow about how she received the new red coat. I shall speak later tonight with her aunt. Now they must go for ice cream, no?"

Sarah was already on her feet and out of her seat. "Let's call Uncle John and have him meet us. After our treats, he can take you to his house and I can come back for my interview. Will that work for you, Detective?"

"*Bien sûr, Mademoiselle.*"

Sarah mouthed a "*merci*" to Vidal, grabbed Miranda's hand, and took off almost running up the aisle.

When Sarah returned from gulping a café and turning Miranda — face-smeared in chocolate ice cream — over to John, most of her newfound friends had already done their police interviews and left. Only Rachel remained, waiting to be called.

"I so, so appreciate everyone rallying round to help

distract Miranda," Sarah said, giving her a hug. "It really meant a lot."

Rachel smiled. "Children are a universal bond." She paused before going on. "It would seem that our lovely Ann-Sophie has been up to her pretty little neck in some sort of skullduggery. Beyond that, no one knows. Or they're not saying."

"How did she die? Where did they find her?" Sarah asked.

"At her sewing table. Silver scissors in her back."

Sarah blanched, a vision of those long sharp blades heading in her own direction a few days before. "Was she wearing an expensive pair of silver shoes?"

Rachel gave her a quizzical frown. "Not that I know of. But an unfriendly sort, that one. Although I put it down to the lack of English."

"Most of the French crew try. We all do," Sarah said. "Oh, woe, so what happens now? Will we still try to proceed with the show?"

Rachel shrugged.

CHAPTER 24

Sarah's turn with Vidal finally came after Rachel emerged from the little anteroom off to the side of the box office that the detective was using for his questioning. "Tell me about this show in London that you three played together," he started out with no preamble.

"Oh, that? It was The Scottish Play, which always brings bad luck," Sarah said, before she'd had a chance to sit down. "But we weren't really in it together. Georgie's ex-husband got kicked out just as we got started."

"And what bad luck did you have with this play, properly named Macbeth, no?"

"Oh," Sarah frowned and shook her head at the detective, "never say that name! But in London, it went fairly smoothly."

"You, personally, had no problems?"

"Well, I got mugged and then burgled, but that had nothing to do with the play. Someone grabbed my purse on the underground."

"I see. And your keys, they were in the handbag?"

"Yeah, worst luck."

At his insistent questioning, she explained that nothing

much was taken that she could remember. "Just a few books, maybe. They threw stuff around. Obviously just kids."

"Did you file a police report?"

"Of course."

He finally got back to the seamstress and the dressing room incident. "Tell me again about the flowers and scissors."

"As I told you before, the attachment for the card had been cut. I assumed it was done with those awful-looking scissors. Ann-Sophie didn't respond; she just said *comment* as though she didn't understand English. And I suspect she took my silver shoes."

He ignored the fashion statement but pressed her on the so-called persons of interest that she'd already told him about: Adeel at the zoo, the library woman, the man in the bowtie at Baudelaire's grave. The only thing new she had to offer was the book she'd found at FNAC with the picture of Bernhardt holding the single-stemmed flowers.

Vidal visibly started at that. "So, the flowers are *bien sûr* directed at you. I have taken care to ask the others only indirectly about flowers. Nothing."

"Do you think Miranda's in danger?"

"I fear, perhaps, yes. The two of you."

CHAPTER 25

It was almost midnight when a fretful Sarah, after picking up her niece at John's, finally got the tired and cranky Miranda home. Vicki and Chess met them at the door, one barking, the other yelling.

"This is it. We have to find another babysitter, and fast. I can*not* jeopardize Miranda's safety anymore. I'm worried about you, too, but I can't fix that. You're grown and should know better."

It went on, but that was its gist. Until, that is, Vicki spotted the so-called kid detective book that Sarah unloaded from her tote bag as she prepared to leave for John's. "What's this? It looks like porn."

Miranda made a grab for it. "It's mine."

"Sarah, where did THIS come from?" Vicki sputtered. "Where?"

"It's a comic book. Miranda wanted it."

"It's mine." Miranda again tried to snatch it from her mother. It indeed was in the over-sized shape of a child's picture book.

"Comic book!" Vicki's voice was a screech. "It has a war

scene on the opening page, and a nude woman smoking a cigarette on the second — a *graphic* novel."

"What's graphic?" Miranda demanded.

A tearful Sarah grabbed up her bag and shot out the front door, leaving behind Chess barking, Vicki yelling, and Miranda crying.

Sarah was still sniffling, half crying and certainly feeling sorry for herself as she turned the key and shoved open the elegant wood door of the place she called home, John and Ben's apartment.

They were seated at the arrangement of low chairs around a glass-topped table in the grand double salon, enjoying a late-evening drink.

"Babe, what's wrong?" John, wearing an encircling caftan of royal blue, braced himself to lumber up from his seat.

Sarah laughed and teared-up at the same time. "I can't understand why you don't have higher chairs. Only short people can get out of those."

John embraced her, engulfing her in a sea of silk. "What is it?"

"It's everything," Sarah sputtered.

"Sit down, sweet thing. Ben'll pour you a drink then tell us."

"Vicki fired me, the play is ruined, and Ann-Sophie has her scissors in her back."

"*Mon Dieu,*" Ben said. "*Whiskey, peut-être?*"

After Sarah filled in the rest of her day's events, John suggested they move to the kitchen with their drinks so she and Ben could sit around the high marble table while John made grilled cheese sandwiches. "Comfort food is what you need."

"Fine. I've something to show you," she said, dragging along her tote bag containing the heavy book with the Rochegrosse pictures.

Perched on a bar stool, Sarah opened her new find, first to the picture that she'd marked with a sticky note.

"Bernhardt, see," she said, stabbing her finger on the image of the actress in a loose-fitting beige silk flecked with red, her masses of auburn locks flowing against an umber backdrop. She was holding a single stem of two white spider mums, exactly like those Sarah had received. "Looks like a snake bracelet on her arm, and perhaps that little crown has a raised-up snake, as well."

"For sure?" John said, coming over from the stove, spatula in hand, the smell of cheese and butter warm in the air. "All your flowers from the same artist?"

"*Bien sûr.*" Ben's voice, low and troubled.

"What does the French say?" Sarah demanded, again stabbing the photo.

"Only of the painting. *Expliqué* why use the *sombre couleurs*. Is to, how you say, make big show of the red hair."

"The somber background makes the hair stand out?" John asked.

"*Oui,*" Ben replied.

"What else is in this book?" John asked, as a sizzle of burning cheese rose from the stove. "Oops, back in a sec."

"So much he is for show biz. *Un pompier,*" Ben said as he began flipping through the volume.

"Yes, you said that before. Did I get it right, a poster artist?" John asked, moving back from the stove with plates of sandwiches.

Ben shrugged. "*Je ne sais pas le mot en anglais.*"

"I guess you've told us enough about what it means. Not well respected by serious French painters. But this is a huge book. He was certainly prolific."

"Qu'est-ce que c'est?"

"Painted a lot," John replied, looking through the tome. "Wow, some of this stuff is pretty violent — a lot based on myth and ancient times. Look at this, *Death of Babylon*, a bunch of nude women lying around in obvious distress among cushions and flowers."

"His message is: 'Death Becomes Her,'" Sarah shuddered. "A fan of this guy's work has got to be sick."

CHAPTER 26

Vicki and the lady detective waited outside the next afternoon for Miranda's school to let out. Vicki, who at five feet two and a half was considered short by most, felt she towered over Elena DuBois, a Hermes scarf perfectly draped over her smartly-cut business suit. Amazing that someone so diminutive could pass whatever physical tests they have for French cops. Made her think of Verhoeven, that midget Parisian police commissioner of best-selling fame who solved bloody, awful murders with the French literary touch that all the crimes were based on well-known but gruesome American novels. Vicki had already called the office about taking a day off to look for a babysitter when Vidal phoned to tell her Miranda was scheduled for a police interview.

Miranda came barreling out with the horde but stopped short when she saw the lady detective, a smile of wonder and excitement spreading over her face. She moved a few steps forward, then stopped again and began sucking her thumb.

"Miranda!" Vicki reached out to nab her awestruck child. Her kid had gone over the top about cops and police. It was way beyond the time when she should have realized this and tried to do something about it. "You remember Detective DuBois. Say hello."

DuBois took Miranda's hand. "Of course, we remember each other. Let's talk as we walk back to your home."

Vicki trailed alongside as Miranda skipped and eagerly responded to the detective's questions about the red mackintosh, all the while sticking to her initial contention that her father had sent it.

Every time the detective countered with, "But your mother says he didn't," Miranda insisted that he had.

"Okay," the detective finally said as they neared their apartment house, "let's go to your home and play a game."

"Yes! Cops and robbers," Miranda said.

The two women made raised-eyebrow contact over Miranda's head. An old refrain played through Vicki's mind, I can't handle this by myself. Her father has got to stay home more and quit chasing wars all over the world.

Upstairs in the living room, coffee and juice at hand, DuBois produced a notebook with pale-blue lines that created tiny squares over an entire blank page.

"This is the way police sketch out a crime scene," she explained to Miranda. "Shall we give it a try?" She drew a line. "Here's the stage. And the entrance to the theater is the other end."

"Wow," Miranda said, "this is fun. When I grow up, I'm going to be a detective just like you."

After much prodding and role playing, it finally boiled down to Miranda's continued insistence that her father had sent the mackintosh, but someone she didn't see had slipped it over her head. She just found herself wearing it. "Then," she said with all-but-foot-stamping indignation, "Aunt Sarah tried to take it away."

Vicki suppressed a grin. Replacing Sarah wasn't going to be as traumatic as she'd feared.

Once the detective left, Vicki put on a cheerful face and bit the bullet, so to speak. "I've arranged for several possible new nannies to come by. We'll talk to them together and see how we like 'em."

Miranda's face clouded over. "I thought now you're my new babysitter. You met me at school."

Vicki grimaced and held back tears. "Oh, baby." She enfolded Miranda, and standing in the hall where they had just bid goodbye to DuBois, they rocked back and forth in each other's arms. *The women who claim you can have it all have never been here*, she thought.

Finally, Miranda broke the moment. "Don't cry, Mommy. A new nanny would be good. I'm tired of Aunt Sarah."

CHAPTER 27

Sarah was moping around John's kitchen earlier that same day, her cell phone in her cut-off jeans pocket, compulsively eating first a croissant then a buttered bagel, one following upon the other, waiting to hear from Gomez. Would he call a meeting, call a rehearsal, or just let them know what the producers planned to do next? She'd been told the voluble director was uncharacteristically evasive after he'd finished his interview with Vidal the night before. "Ve'll see," he'd responded to every question from cast members.

When the ring came, Sarah jumped and let out an involuntary squeal upsetting the current bagel, butter side down, on John's spotless floor.

Unhappily, it wasn't Gomez but Detective Vidal wanting to meet with her right away.

Sarah had no luck putting the cop off. "I shall come shortly."

When she politely offered the code for her downstairs door, weariness in his voice, Vidal replied, "*Merci*, but I have arrived there before."

After finishing the call, Sarah noticed the Rochegrosse art book still lying open on the table. Should she show it to

Vidal? She had told him about it, already mentioned the white Bernhardt flowers she'd received. No sense in giving the cop more to quiz her about. This was something she and Ben could follow up on their own. He'd said the night before that he would check around with art scholars to see if they knew of anyone obsessed with the artist. But before she could decide, the doorbell rang.

Vidal refused her offer of coffee and croissant, saying he couldn't linger and had only a few questions. They stood in the kitchen as he talked. "I have report from the London police. They say books were stolen."

Sarah was bewildered. "What are you talking about?"

"The collected poetry of Henry Van Dyke."

"Who?"

"*Bien sûr*, I don't know," Vidal replied. "London said he was American."

"You mean the robbery at my London apartment? I have no idea. Maybe something left over from college. I took a lot of stuff when I went there for a theater internship."

"When the report said books of *poésies*, I asked more details. I thought surely they would say Baudelaire. *Mais non*, they said the work of *le français* was not among those things that you reported stolen. Some clothes, you thought, perhaps old shoes and gymnasium costumes."

"Exactly," Sarah said. "It must have been kids. I think there was a hooded sweatshirt."

"Sweatshirt?" Vidal looked quizzical.

"You know," Sarah held her arms loosely around her chest then extended them over her head. "Mine had a UC logo."

Vidal just rolled his eyes.

The call had finally come, and Sarah was hurrying up the rue du Temple to Gomez's apartment. She felt empty-handed without Miranda tagging along chattering. She'd gotten a text from Vicki this morning saying she'd taken the day off to interview babysitters. "I'm sorry," Vicki had signed off nicely, "but you have too much going on in your life to have time to worry about picking Miranda up at school." That was putting as nice a face on it as possible, Sarah decided. Her older sister had always been protective of her. Critical, for sure, but always protective.

But now, without her family wanting or needing her any more, did she really care whether or not she stayed in Paris? John loved her, and he and Ben seemed happy enough to have her staying with them, but that had to be a short-term arrangement. She'd excitedly grabbed at the idea of an English-language show so she could be here with her sister and beloved niece. When the production was threatened, she'd been willing to fight to keep it going. But now? Pointless! Yet, where would she go? What would she do?

Caught up in her thoughts, she nearly bumped into an odd man in a three-piece suit. "I beg your pardon, Madame," he said in a cultivated British accent, tipping his bowler hat. A bowler hat! Sarah giggled. Weird. And a rather hot day for worsted wool. Already September, but the oppressive heat of August was receding at a foot-dragging pace.

Sarah rushed on into the foyer of Gomez's building and winced at the sight of the elevator call button. She teared-up for an instant, seeing in her mind's eye her adorable little button-pusher on tiptoe reaching, then bit down hard on her back teeth and admonished herself to get a grip. She could hardly afford to arrive upstairs crying. They'd think she was worried about the fate of this silly, stupid show. Damn, her life was a mess!

But there was an excited stir in the apartment when she entered. "Gomez says we're going forward." Even the placid, even-tempered Rachel delivered the news with what for her was a shout.

"What brought that on?" Sarah asked into the hubbub but got no response.

"Where's Gomez?" She made her voice bigger.

"On the phone with the producers," Paul, the waiter, yelled from across the room. "Have a drink."

Humph, he's certainly staying in character, Sarah thought. Several wine bottles and glasses sat on a table off to the side accompanied by nearly depleted bowls of peanuts and some wilted-looking paper napkins. They surely were left over from the night before, too early in the day for this.

Sommes laughed as he saw Sarah surveying the sparse party offerings. "Always the big-spending host," he quipped.

"Ladies and gentlemen!" Gomez materialized, took the room's center, and began speaking in a rush. "Is decided. Producers say ve must proceed, don't care who plays what part. They say just roll. Publicity too good. Third murder will pack houses in London and New York. Ve rehearse now. Ve haf winner!"

"No turning back," Sommes said, awe in his voice. "So what about the casting?"

"Margery is wife and Sarah is psychic."

"Our Mag agreed to stay, thinking she'll finally make it to the West End," Sommes snipped.

Sarah winced. In the killer's sights again!

"I am in blood stepped in so far," she said, almost to herself, "that I should wade no more."

CHAPTER 28

Sarah walked slowly home from Gomez's through the dusty pink of an arriving nightfall as the city's fairytale street lights began to wink on.

What was happening in her life? Where had the red mackintosh come from? Why did it make Miranda act so crazy? Could there be some kind of chemical in the rubberized fabric that caused the kid's wild behavior when wearing the coat? Or was it simply a child-like expression of missing her father? Sarah thought of her own beloved dad — killed in a crash on a Los Angeles freeway by a drunk, speeding in and out of home-bound cars. Sarah was twelve. She'd been awakened by police arriving to notify the family — nightmares for years about that knock on the door.

Was Miranda somehow acting out the equivalent of Sarah's bad dreams? Sarah's father had called her Princess even before that fateful Halloween dress-up day when Vicki renamed her show-off kid sister after the great Miss Bernhardt. Little Suzie from then on was Sarah. Vicki meant it as a joke, but for Sarah it was deliverance into a new persona at the age of five. She was an actress from then on — occupied her own place in the world with a special identity that belonged to no one but her.

She picked up speed threading her way through the strollers and sidewalk drinkers on the narrow Street of the Old Temple. She smiled mischievously to herself. Who cares if others see me as dreamy, ditzy. I've got a role to play, and that's myself. Why, she'd often asked her mother, had she been named Suzie instead of, at least, a serious Susan?

"I thought Suzie was cute," her mother always replied as Sarah ground her teeth in despair at the concept of "cute." She finally legally changed her name to Sarah to eliminate passport and school transcript problems.

But what was going on with Miranda? Nearly the same young age as Sarah when she found her life's work, forever knowing who she was. The child missed her roving correspondent father — never home, if one listened to Vicki complaining about his absence. Yet Miranda endlessly quoted "Daddy," which gave one the impression that she spent a great deal of time with him. It was hard for Sarah to judge, since Bill had been gone during the few weeks she'd been in Paris.

Sarah passed by the huge Archives Nationales that gave its name to John's street as she neared home. At least it was her home for now. Abandoned by her niece, she'd been ready to leave Paris, but she was back once again in the crosshairs.

CHAPTER 29

The three of them sat on high stools at their favorite gathering spot — the round, marble table in John's kitchen, he snapping at Sarah. "This is nuts. You can't keep risking your life," he groused.

"I can't quit now." Sarah threw her arms wide. "The play's the thing. It's in my DNA. I could never do that."

John scowled. "Yeah, well you certainly can emote, regardless."

Sarah grew a small pout. "What does that mean?"

"That whatever the situation, you're always on stage." John's was the face of gloom, and his heart felt sore. He rarely got angry with this sweet, blithe spirit, but his patience had reached its limits.

"That's who I am," she wailed. "What else can I do?"

Ben watched the two of them, as though at a tennis match, head swiveling from one to the other, his eyes growing wider, a perplexed frown on his face. "Perhaps we have *un verre*," he finally ventured.

"Yes. This definitely calls for wine," John growled. "Or maybe something stronger."

Ben slid from his stool and began gathering glasses and

bottles then stopped in mid pour when, out of the blue, Sarah asked what John knew about van Dyck.

"Van Dyck?" John's face mirrored the perplexity on Ben's. "The Flemish artist? Don't tell me you've gotten flowers that look like *his* paintings?"

"You speak of *le flamand*?" Ben said. "*Je ne comprends pas.* He was not for many flowers."

Sarah frowned. "Detective Vidal said he was a poet."

"Poet? You sure? Why would he ask about that?" John demanded.

"The collected poetry of Henry van Dyke. That's what he said. Then he wrote it down."

"So?" John was more than weary of this whole business.

"Vidal said he was an American," Sarah insisted. "He said he'd expected Baudelaire because, I guess, of the guy with the plastic bowtie."

"Sarah, babe, stop and think. You're not making any sense. Why did Vidal say this to you?"

"How should I know? This morning, he calls and rushes over and starts talking about the London police. When I was robbed. The only connection I could see with anything was the play I was in back then. The Scottish Play. With Georgie. Vidal claimed I told the police a volume of poetry was stolen plus some old gym shoes. Kids, I told them. And him."

John had stopped listening and was searching on his mobile. "Henry, you said. Not Anthony? Right?"

"I think so."

"Yeah. Well here he is. American poet, 1852-1933. Died in Princeton, where he was an English professor. Nothing to do with the Flemish painter. Different spelling. Beard though, looks like the one named for the painter."

"What's any of this got to do with me?" Sarah whined.

"For god's sake, Sarah," John snapped. "Vidal apparently said you told the London police you had a book of his poetry."

"Really?" She looked startled. "But that was so long ago. Probably some college text that I never even read."

"*Très compliqué*," Ben said as he moved over to the fridge and pulled out a second bottle of wine.

"I told them it must have been kids," Sarah said again. "They scrawled graffiti on the wall. 'Americans go home.'"

"Wow," John said, immersed in his scrolling. "One of his poems was read at Princess Diana's funeral."

"You're kidding." Sarah reached for the phone. "Let me see."

John ducked her reach and read:

> **Time is too slow for those who wait,**
> **Too swift for those who fear,**
> **Too long for those who grieve,**
> **Too short for those who rejoice,**
> **But for those who love,**
> **Time is not.**

John took another swig of wine, and continued scrolling. "Christ," he said.

"What?" Sarah grabbed at the phone, but he brushed her hand away.

"Another of his poems. Listen to this:

> **'So it's home again, home again, America for me.**
> **My heart is turning home again,**
> **and there I long to be.'"**

"*Mon Dieu*." Ben seemed to expel the words rather than say them, as Sarah's mouth flew open, but nothing came out except "American."

Now, there were four on the high stools around the small marble table. Glasses were full, empty bottles lined the kitchen counters like so many silent, fallen soldiers.

"I'm way behind," Mary said, downing the last of what was her first glass. "You should have called me sooner."

"It didn't take long after we realized it was poetry we were talking about. You're the expert. It just took you too long to get here." John was already slurring his words a little.

Mary laughed. "At least Ben is still sober. The French have the good sense to not get drunk on wine. Damned Anglo-Saxons don't know better."

"So, okay. What do you know about Henry van Dyke?" John asked.

Mary laughed again. "Probably way less than you already know from Wikipedia. If he's an American, not my field. I just never want to miss a party. Or a sleuthing session. Whatever this is meant to be."

"Ah, *quelle dommage*," Ben said. "We hope for you knowing on *les poètes. Peut-être Sarah et moi* must go to search the few of Rochegrosse in Paris."

"Sounds a plan. So what's the state of play on the rest of it? Bring me up to date. Sarah's back to work again. What else?"

"We thought you'd know everything," Sarah said. "That your detective would have told you."

Mary frowned. "I keep telling you that he's not my boyfriend. We've been out to dinner once, and he came with me to see the play where your second actress — or was it the third? — got murdered. You keep him so busy with killings, Sarah, he doesn't have time for a social life."

Sarah's face clouded over. "Oh, Mary, I'm so sorry."

John laughed. "Babe, when will you ever learn not to fall

for Mary's blarney. She's never happier playing the cynic or pulling someone's leg."

"Fine. Get on with it. So what *is* the state of play?" Mary grinned and shoved her glass in Ben's direction. "*Un autre verre, s'il te plait.*"

"Indeed," John said. "Let's get on with it."

"The worst thing is that Vicki fired me."

"Fired?" Mary looked startled.

"No," John interrupted. "The worst thing is that another woman was murdered. The seamstress."

CHAPTER 30

Mary was looking around John's shop the next morning, waiting for Ben and Sarah, remembering the chaos here when John was robbed and she'd found him trussed up, stuck in the old-fashioned, makeshift water closet. Was it really only a couple of weeks ago?

That crime got solved, thanks in part to the lovely fellow, J.C. Vidal. She smiled. The detective was, indeed, a special man. She'd even begun to get over feeling guilty about the attraction, a widow of only a few months, as she was. But the violence continued. What creepy thing was going on? Two more murders, or was it three, since the death of the first actress, what was her name? She'd had a real name and a phony one, as Mary remembered it. The point being, though, the woman was an MI6 agent planted in Sarah's acting troupe. So now, Sarah says, some of her fellow actors are once again suspecting professional spies are at the root of the latest troubles.

The tiny brass bell over the door tinkled, and John moved forward to greet a customer. Mary loved this spot with its eclectic collection of oil paintings, antique Louis XV dibs and dabs, and whatever else might catch the eye of a visitor cruising art galleries and fashionable stores under the archways encircling the green square of the Place des Vosges.

But where were Ben and Sarah? Mary was getting restless. She'd already sniffed around and inspected any new acquisitions, beamed at the still-here Klee of bright orange and yellows, and wanted to now get a move on. Sarah had somehow extracted a promise from Ben to pry himself from his studio as guide for her to view the few Rochegrosse paintings on public display in the city. John had asked Mary to go with them because "Ben's English isn't all that good, and trying to decipher constant quotes from the Bard won't make it any easier."

Definitely an understatement. The flighty actress strained Mary's nerves but amused her all the same. Mary was also gob-smacked that Sarah had been taken off the babysitting roster. The willful kid and the spacey actress seemed such a splendid fit. Even the Lady Gaga T-shirt made sense, a normal kid would be a fan of Taylor Swift.

Speaking of — here she came wearing a big floppy hat and platform heels that anyone short of perfect balance would fall off straight away. Perhaps aerobatics was part of the trade. Old-timey actors used to do a lot of sword fighting, so probably acrobatics or dancing were part of Sarah's training as well. Vicki had bragged that her kid sister worked hard to prepare for the classical stage — London interning and the lot.

"All hail!" Sarah pronounced as she stepped inside. John's customer, a heavy-set woman in khaki shorts and baseball cap turned from her examination of an antique chair to peer over her half glasses in wonderment.

"Saints be praised," Mary said, "a new source. What became of Lady Macbeth?"

Sarah smiled. "I'm well versed."

Mary laughed. "Got me there. So where are we off to?"

"Ben is our leader," Sarah said, waving her arm to give him direction. "Hie us hence."

"I give up." Mary shook her head. "I'm supposed to translate for Ben, but I'm way out of my depth."

Sarah waltzed over to give John a peck on the cheek before moving toward the door.

"I'm surprised," Mary quipped, "that you could fit him in under that big hat."

As the three of them scooted out, Mary heard the lady in shorts ask John, "Is she someone famous?"

"So, Ben, I did my homework before I got here," Mary said. "We're headed for the Orsay, no?"

"*Oui,*" Ben replied. *"Ce musée* angers me, but is only one, I think, with Rochegrosse. The grand *Chevalier aux Fleurs.*"

"Let's taxi then — queue just past the Café Hugo at the top of the street," she said pointing up the block.

"This *Knight of the Flowers,*" Mary continued, "according to the Orsay Web site, is from the Arthurian legend."

"Oui. You are correct."

"That guy in armor surrounded by women and pretty flowers?" Sarah asked. "Practically the only happy painting in the book."

"A bit weird, I'd say," Mary grumbled. "A chaste knight standing among nude virgins frolicking in posies. With the violence in other of his paintings, I'd venture that a fan of this Rochegrosse has ambivalent feelings toward women."

Ben beamed. "Yes. Mary says it well."

"Creepy," Sarah said. "But is that chevalier the young knight of King Arthur? The one who found the Holy Grail?"

"Yep," Mary replied. "The same. Sir Percivale. Again, the Orsay site calls the painting *Parsifal* — references Wagnerian operas dealing with old myths and legends that inspired artists of that generation."

"A rose by any other name," Sarah giggled.

"You'd know," Mary said. "You're the one getting the flowers."

A mist of water sprayed by whirling fans, the French idea of air-conditioning, wafted over from the sidewalk café as the three friends lined up in the taxi queue. "Maybe we could go get Miranda. She loves the museum," Sarah said.

Ben frowned. "No time, I must return soon to my studio."

"Maybe the new babysitter could bring her there," Sarah persisted.

Mary laughed. "You don't need your midget translator. You've got me."

"Let's just call Vicki," Sarah insisted. "Maybe she'll say yes."

As a taxi pulled up, Ben reached out to open the door for the ladies, but a mustachioed man in a deerstalker hat beat him to it. With a wave, he grabbed the door handle, tipped his hat, and made a sweeping bow. "For your pleasure, Madame."

The three climbed in, Ben told the driver the Musée d'Orsay, and off they sped.

"Strange custom," Sarah said, "a doorman at a taxi stand?"

Ben and Mary burst out laughing.

"What's so funny?"

"He was flirting with you," Mary said. "Ben and I were wallpaper."

"You attract the men. *Bien sûr*," Ben said.

"A Brit, quite an upper-class accent, not to mention

the headgear," Mary replied. "An old flame from London, perhaps?"

"Of course not. Don't be silly. But that's the second guy in a strange hat I've run in to the last two days."

Sarah turned away and pulled her mobile from her handbag to dial Vicki.

Mary felt an unexpected twinge of sympathy, hearing the plea in Sarah's voice.

"Mary and Ben will be with us. They won't let us get into harm."

When a beaming Sarah finally got off the phone, the pleading had morphed to joy. "Vicki said Miranda's pretty listless, after just one day doesn't like the new sitter, pouting that she's no fun. And the poor babe drew a picture and mailed it to the police lady at the station house but hasn't heard back. Vicki's going to tell the sitter to get a taxi and bring Miranda to meet us at the museum."

As they pulled up to the old train station turned museum, the big black hands of its grand see-through clock pointing to the hour, Mary spotted Miranda in a proper pleated skirt, knee sox, and shiny patent Mary Janes. A stern-looking middle-aged French woman had a tight grip on her arm.

The first thing the kid said when they got out of the cab was, "I wanted to wear my Lady Gaga T-shirt, but Madame le Clerc wouldn't let me."

Sarah lunged for a grand hug, but Miranda shied away.

CHAPTER 31

The entry lines snaked around the block, but Ben showed his Painters Society membership card, and the four of them scooted right in.

Just past the ticket takers, he grabbed the first person wearing a badge and asked where they could find *Le Chevalier* painting. Negative head shake. The next badge-wearer lighted up. "Yes, I remember. A big oil. Near an entranceway in the old book shop. But the store was moved and that exit closed because of terrorism precautions." He frowned. "Don't know what they did with the painting."

"So, who does know?" Ben snapped.

Translating for Sarah, as they moved fast following Ben around while he made one sharp-toned query after another, Mary noticed that Sarah was keeping in lockstep with Miranda, who'd been shy of her aunt at first. But after a couple of attempts at taking her niece's hand, Sarah finally managed a détente. The kid seemed to realize that it was relent or run the risk of getting lost as the four of them sped through the confusing old train station with its many balconies and galleries.

Mary had never seen Ben cranky before, but he certainly was now. "*Le musée* has many lately of *exhibitions* of distaste. *Sur le crime* and *la punition*." He ranted on. Only a few intelligible words, English or French, would rise up through the froth. Sarah wore a perpetually startled look. Miranda clearly was interested and trying to follow, but Mary knew that if she herself couldn't keep up the four-year-old, no matter how excellent her bilingual abilities, was at sea as well.

Ben was speaking so fast in his anger that she wanted to implore him to use French, and she would translate. His English was all but impossible to follow.

"*Tout ce nonsense*, they place in storage *quelque chose* good enough to list on the web as in collection. So much lost time."

Poor guy, Mary thought, *frustrated he's not back at his*

*studio getting ready for his own exhibition instead of dragging
Sarah et al around on this thankless quest.*

"We're getting into an arcane battle of the art historians,"
Mary explained to Sarah, "that has nothing to do with us."
She stopped, frowned, then offered, "Unless, perhaps, this
flower sender of yours is in the camp of reviving what some
are calling kitsch and is expressing it this way."

"Should we tell Detective Vidal then?" Sarah asked.

Mary's face lit up with a mischievous grin. "Hmm, good
excuse for me to invite him to dinner."

"I thought you were trying to discourage him," Sarah said
in surprise.

"Who knows what I've got in mind. Certainly not me."

After still another enquiry, it was off to an administrative
office where computer buttons were pushed and Ben paced.
"Yes. It was loaned in 2013 for an exhibit in Moulins but has
been in storage since. Sorry, but the Chevalier is not currently
on exhibit."

Ben exploded at the bureaucrat in rapid French, then
turned to Mary and Sarah. "*Ce musée* becomes *ridicule*."
Sarah shot Mary a look. "What?" she said, as Ben returned to
excoriating the officials his voice low and scathing.

"The one decent example of this kind of kitsch is not on
view." Mary was stumbling with the translation for Sarah.
"Meanwhile, you go to the depths of exhibits on prostitution,
crime and punishment, the guillotine. It's an outrage."

"Come, ladies," Ben beckoned and stormed out.

Mary glanced at the man holding open the office door.
He didn't have a mustache and was sporting an artist's beret
instead of a deerstalker cap, yet he still seemed like that taxi
valet. He had a wide grin over a slightly red upper lip and made

an odd little bow. Had he followed them from the Marais? No, he'd have to have shaved on the way. Something false ripped off? She swiveled to Sarah, and they exchanged questioning frowns over Miranda's head.

Sarah had the child's hand, and the three of them were almost running to keep up as Ben moved onto an escalator descending into the mid-day sun streaming through the glass-domed ceiling arching over the exhibition hall.

"Why do we have to go?" Miranda demanded. "They have flan in the café, and I like to look at Sacre Coeur through the clock."

CHAPTER 32

During the cab ride to John's, Miranda chattered nonstop about things she and Daddy did when they went to the Orsay — all of it clearly aimed at the present adults who didn't know how to do things right and have fun.

Home from work for a few weekday chores, John greeted them at the door, startled they were back so soon. Ben brushed past him and hurried down the hall toward his studio.

John started to follow but stopped short in the kitchen, looking at the bags of unopened groceries he hadn't had time to put away.

"We don't know what's gotten into him," Sarah said, right on his heels. "Mary thinks it's kitsch. Me thinks he doth protest too much."

"I should have known, with your going to the Orsay," John replied.

"What the devil does that mean?" Mary asked. "You knew it was doomed from the start?"

"In the back of my mind, I guess." John was repentant.

"I didn't understand the point of looking at the painting, anyway," Mary groused. "You saw it in the book."

"Yes, I guess it wasn't too well thought out," John admitted

135

with a slight frown. "I just wanted Ben to get out of the studio for a while and distract Sarah from worrying about her role. So what exactly happened?"

"Nothing," Sarah said. "That was the problem."

"We went everywhere asking for a picture, but Ben got mad," Miranda said, climbing up on a high stool at the marble table. "We didn't get to look at anything or eat flan. May I have some apple juice, please."

John patted her head. "Sure, little one. Uncle John's happy to see you back in the fold." He looked over at Sarah. "I guess that's another story I need to hear."

He moved around the kitchen, setting up glasses and pulling things from the fridge as he talked. "Ben's railed about the Orsay for a long time. A few years ago, they got a new curator who started with these attention-grabbing exhibits that moved the more staid Impressionists upstairs. Much of the new stuff seems salacious or gory. It culminated several years ago with a real guillotine dragged out of storage."

"Yeah, that was quite the sensation," Mary injected. "Thousands of viewers, including lots of school kids. The thing was draped in some kind of gauze."

"Ben hasn't been back," John said. "He never forgave them. Images of body parts, severed heads."

"That was the exhibit?" Sarah asked.

"Oh, no," John said. "There were tons of important art works in the display. But the guillotine gave lots of people apoplexy. Sorry about the wasted day."

"Not for me." Sarah was glowing. "Miranda's back with us. She didn't like her new nanny."

"Madame le Clerc was too old," Miranda said.

"Old?" John asked.

"She didn't like to have fun."

"So, who do you like to have fun with?" Sarah reached over playfully to tickle her niece.

"Aunt Sarah." Miranda laughed and squealed. "Let's go to the skeleton museum. You said we could."

"Absolutely." Sarah grinned. And to John's uplifted questioning eyebrows: "Vicki said at least until rehearsals start. The cops have the theater again."

She picked up the glass of juice John offered and continued, "So Mary and I saw this same man again. Maybe we should tell Detective Vidal."

"What same man?" John asked. "Talk about a change of subject."

"You know, the one at the taxi stop."

"No, I don't know," John said in exasperation. "What are you talking about?"

"Tell him Mary. Nobody ever believes me."

CHAPTER 33

Looking for the way out, Sarah realized the metro had not been a good idea. She and Miranda were quite lost. Not just trying to find the proper exit, but from wandering one wrong, dank corridor then another. They'd take a turn down a long, empty hall only to veer off to a new one streaming with rushing commuters from what seemed to be the stop for a giant rail station. Next time she would ask John how to take a bus. Staying above ground felt like a wiser thing to do — especially now that Vicki had admonished her once again about Miranda's safety. "I must be an awful mother to allow my child back with you. But she was miserable with that rigid French matron. I can't bear to see her so unhappy. She missed your games. I swear, I don't know which of you is the younger."

"The skeleton museum is that way," Miranda was much surer of herself than Sarah felt. These tunnels were creepy. "There's a sign."

"Can you read it?" Sarah asked.

"No. But …"

"But what?" Sarah snapped. "It's got an arrow on it?"

A rushing woman with very high heels and an even tighter skirt, stopped abruptly.

"Un problème?" she asked Sarah.

"Oui, merci," Miranda replied. *"Le Jardin des Plantes, si vous plaît."*

The woman pointed to a distant staircase and rushed on.

Trudging up the smelly flight, Sarah rejoiced at the sight ahead — a cloudless sky. Light at the end of a tunnel! A man in a pinstriped business suit, carrying a battered briefcase, brushed past them on the way up with no *"pardonnez-moi,"* nearly colliding with a woman on the way down carrying a child's stroller, a kid tagging at the back of her skirt.

Finally. Feet on the sidewalk, solid ground. Miranda pointed excitedly across a wide boulevard of whizzing cars, "the *jardin*." An immense, tranquil green space dotted with trees, flowers, several large official-looking buildings, and people ambling along or sitting on benches.

"This is quite a different entry point than when we visited the zoo," Sarah said.

"Oh, yes," Miranda replied in her instructive, talking-down-to-her-aunt voice. "It's a very large garden."

But how to get across what was almost a speedway? It intersected with a traffic circle, a bridge crossing, a rail station entrance, and a parking spot for idling city buses. Sarah cursed herself for not asking about a bus. She had to start paying more attention.

Walking toward the river, it appeared to Sarah that no matter how she tried to sort out the scattered stoplights, crossing boiled down to a carnival game of dodger cars.

"There's a place," Miranda finally yelled. And sure enough, near the train station inroad, white stripes in the street marked a way across.

As they entered a leafy pathway, Sarah glimpsed first the

battered briefcase then saw the man. He was wearing a snap-brimmed hat she hadn't noticed before, shading the upper half of his face. Stones have been known to move and trees to speak. And then he was gone.

Could that have been the man she was beginning to think of as the master-of-disguise? The guy who just seemed to pop up wherever she was? This would be the fourth time in the last two days: at the taxi stop, when leaving the Orsay, and on her way to the meeting at Gomez's yesterday. He looked completely different each time, yet still somehow recognizable. Always a distinctive hat! CIA flashed in her head. In his business suit and pulled-down brim, he did resemble a G-Man.

Some in the cast kept insisting that feds were involved in Georgie's murder. Sarah had discounted such fantastical talk. Just because the first murdered actress was some sort of British spy didn't mean Georgie was. But this nondescript guy seemed to fit the bill. Even his attaché case was scuffed. Why, though, follow me? Of what importance could I be? Unless it's the role I've stepped into! Someone with a grudge against the play, the company, the role? Kill whoever is playing the blind psychic? Could blindness somehow have something to do with it? Sarah shuddered.

She tightened her grip on Miranda's hand. She had to protect her niece. The guy had been watching them. Maybe he was a child molester and had nothing to do with the play. Sarah resolved to start acting like a detective. Or even better! The scheming Lady Macbeth. Now there was one tough broad. Screw your courage to the sticking place. With that kind of outlook, Sarah could take on the world! The heck with that peeping Tom. She wasn't going to be intimidated by some two-bit gumshoe.

"There it is," Miranda yelled and pointed. "The skeleton museum."

Sure enough. A reddish stone Victorian with huge, leaded windows. And, Oh my God, leaning against a column at its entryway, large as life with a big grin, was Adeel. Sarah blinked. He had on a suit but no briefcase. No way could he be the man they'd just seen. Or could he? She studied Adeel's face. She'd sort of forgotten what he looked like. A master of disguise could have tossed the slouch hat, but it wasn't the same suit — couldn't have changed that fast. Sarah had emailed Adeel, giving in against her better judgment to Miranda's whining, suggesting that they meet after the skeleton museum for cakes at the mosque. She had definitely said the mosque, not here. And she certainly hadn't mentioned flowers. Flowers! Enough already. That was indeed a rose in his hand, done up in cellophane with a bow!

Sarah's heart raced. She was all but positive Adeel couldn't be the man in disguise. But he *was* a suspect. Vicki would kill her. Probably so would John. Detective Vidal, as well. They'd all told her in one way or another to be careful. Vidal had specifically said to stay clear of any of his so-called suspects. Adeel was right up there with the Baudelaire fan wearing the plastic bowtie. Now she'd not only have to act like she was happy about the flowers but take a picture as well so Ben could check if they were still another replication from those awful paintings. Sarah's mind clicked through violent images of roiling, naked women in the book she'd bought at FNAC — a single rose was tame compared to the slideshow in her head.

"Hi," Miranda yelled, breaking loose from Sarah's hand and running headlong to greet the pleasant, almost bland, but handsome young Parisian the kid'd taken to calling "the Cookie Man."

"You're quite early," Sarah said, catching up. "Miranda and I wanted some quiet time in the museum." Hardly a friendly greeting, and definitely no smile. But let the oaf know right off that they had their guard up, were not about to be kidnapped, or whatever awful thing he had in mind!

His smile faded. Good. He got the point. The outstretched rose fell to his side in a limp hand.

"Sorry," he mumbled. "I had some free time."

At least he had the good grace to be embarrassed. Would a killer be so easily foiled? And, how now to accept the rose? She had to get a picture.

She pondered his face again. Surely, he couldn't be the weird fellow who kept popping up all over the place.

"I had thought," Adeel said so quietly that Sarah had to strain to hear, "that perhaps the young mademoiselle might like a ride on a dinosaur. After you had made a visit to *le musée*."

"Oh, I love dinosaurs. Just like my book, *Danny and the Dinosaur*."

Sarah's heart did a flip as she watched Miranda gleefully sidling up to Adeel. The guy sure knew how to make a play for the kid. Dinosaurs indeed! She had to get a picture of the rose then get him out of here. But a rose was a rose. How different could it be? "*Monsieur* Adeel," Sarah's voice was close to shaking, "perhaps we can meet you somewhere later."

Calling him "mister" was plainspoken, and it registered as two bright red spots on Adeel's cheeks. "Of course," he said. "We could rendezvous at *le Dodo Manège*, the carousel of extinct animals."

Miranda looked from one to the other, a perplexed frown spreading. "Why?"

Adeel, the wrapped rose still hanging limply by his side, took his leave as Sarah managed a quick picture with her cell phone.

CHAPTER 34

Mary was out of breath as she rushed up the metro steps at Châtelet. She and Vidal had agreed to meet for a quick coffee at the Bernhardt Bistro. In Mary's mind, this was theater central with two of Paris's main showcases facing each other across the square dominated by a gilded Napoleonic Goddess of Victory. Mary had never been in the cafe, but it was Sarah's favorite hangout. She'd suggested it when she asked Mary to inform Vidal about the man of many disguises.

Mary glanced around the outdoor tables, before spotting Vidal in an inside corner smiled down upon by a languid Bernhardt. Photos and posters of the great actress, svelte and fierce, in everything from ball gowns to battle dress lined the walls. The first thing Vidal said was, "I was happy to hear your call." Delivered with a big smile.

Mary felt the heat of blush move up her neck to take residence in her warm cheeks.

"Yes," she replied, "I'm…"

I'm what? she wondered. For one, flustered. I'm also a grown woman, a young widow. What is it about this guy that puts me at such odds with myself?

"I'm here," she sputtered out, "to fill you in on the man of many disguises, or at least that's what Sarah calls him. She wanted me to tell you, even had me spell it out to John. She says people always think she traffics in too much imagination."

Vidal grinned with an affirmative nod, then Mary laughed.

"Good," she said, "that breaks the ice."

A waiter deposited two steamy, tiny Espresso cups. "*C'est tout?*" he asked.

Vidal lifted a brow at Mary.

"Thank you," she hesitated. "Nothing more. I can't stay long."

"So, to the man in disguise," Mary said, with a getting-down-to-business finality. "I saw someone twice, who I think was the same bloke yet looked very different each time. Sarah claims at least two more. She just texted that she and Miranda had seen him at the Austerlitz metro on their way to the Jardin de Plantes."

"Mary," Vidal said, placing his hand in easy reach of hers across the small bistro table, "I am unquiet about you ladies. No one appears to take caution."

"Just what would you have us do? Sarah is irrepressible, and the rest of us need to live our lives." She cocked her head slightly then conjured a sly smile. "Perhaps the police could provide a guard for Miranda like they did before?"

Vidal shook his head. "That was such a time when a kidnap threatened the child."

Mary paused, then with a touch of exasperation, continued. "I don't know what else I could do other than begin to surreptitiously follow Sarah when she's supposed to be looking after the child."

"*Mon Dieu*, please no. Already, I have disquiet for you."

"I appreciate the concern, Detective. But these are my friends."

"I have said before, my name is Jean, not 'Detective.'"

She touched his hand. "Thank you. It's been a while since anyone was very worried about me."

"Perhaps you must take me also as one of your friends."

CHAPTER 35

Miranda was whining and dragging her feet as they mounted the steps to the Gallery of Paleontology and Comparative Anatomy.

"You're mean as Madame le Clerc. The Cookie Man was going to help me ride a dinosaur."

"We'll go there after." Sarah was tamping down anger, trying to focus on how much she'd missed the minx while she was out of her life. "You've been clamoring to see the skeletons."

"What's clamoring?"

"Demanding, asking for." Sarah smiled down at her niece and took her hand. All was right with the world.

They passed through a marbled rotunda and Sarah gasped. "Oh my god!"

Heading straight at them was a stampeding herd of skeletal animals, their bleached bones and empty eye-sockets shimmering in sunlight that flooded the vast hall from overhead windows.

"Oh my god," she said again.

Miranda burbled. "It's my favorite thing!"

From minuscule to mammoth, elephants and giraffes,

baboons, dogs, whales, and hippopotami formed a parade of white ribcages down the center of the building. Smaller skeletons were in front, the colossi bringing up the rear, heightening the sense of impending stampede. The tiny specimens were in glass cabinets lining the walls.

Aunt and niece moved in awe up one side and down the other, with Miranda explaining at each wonder what Daddy had explained to her. "Maybe," she said, frowning, as they came toward the end of a long row, "I should wait to go ride the dinosaur with Daddy. He might be disappointed if I saw something he didn't know about."

Finally, locating a bench for rest and a gulp of water from the bottle in her purse, Sarah also fished out a brochure in English.

"It says there are extinct animals on the second floor. Dinosaurs, surely," she said, waving the paper.

"No, I want to ride one! And you said we could have cakes at the mosque."

Sarah shrugged. Might as well go to the ride. Adeel couldn't hurt them out in the open, and it would give her more information for Vidal. She had to start finding clues to these murders!

When they'd found their way to the Dodo Manège, Miranda broke away from Sarah's hand and began a dash around the carousel. A goofy-looking thing. Dominated by yellow, spotted animals that vaguely resembled flying horses, there was also a huge ostrich-like bird with a gray body and a very long pink neck, and a disproportionally large lion with an extremely full, mangy-looking mane.

"Delighted that you were able to come." Adeel popped up

at Sarah's elbow, the miscreant rose nowhere in evidence, the now familiar Cheshire grin filling his face.

A touch of chill swept across Sarah on the warm day.

"I can't find the dinosaur." Miranda skidded in with a cloud of dust akin to a slide into home plate. "This place is no good, or Daddy would have brought me here."

"Dinosaur? I beg your pardon," Adeel said. "I only meant something old. I think there are only birds and turtles and extinct giraffes."

"Turtles." Miranda's face was a study in disgust. "I don't want to ride a turtle."

"My mistake." Adeel frowned. "I had thought dinosaur was an English word for something ancient."

Again, that Brit accent Sarah had detected when they first met. "When was it that you studied in London, Adeel?"

He looked startled. "I spent a year there. I began English in primary school but went to London to perfect it. Why do you ask?"

"Just curious if it might have been last year. About the same time I was there."

"Yes, quite. That's when I was there as well." His face lighted up at what he likely took as a play for his attention. "A nice coincidence, that."

Same time she was in London! Sarah glowed, feeling like a real sleuth. Lady Macbeth, Private Eye, indeed! She couldn't wait to tell Vidal. This would certainly make up for her having contacted Adeel in the first place. Now she must get them out of here, and quick.

"Let's go," she said to her niece.

"No. I want to ride something."

"But I thought you said you didn't like this place because your father doesn't know about it."

"I'll show him as a surprise when he gets home. And you said we could go for cakes at the mosque. Monsieur Adeel promised."

"Yes, quite." The Cheshire grin stepped in. "I've told the young mademoiselle I'd be most happy to escort her any time."

Miranda brightened. "My daddy usually takes me. He likes the cakes too."

Trouble brewing. One minute the kid was annoyed because Adeel had messed up on the dinosaurs, now she was being seduced by desserts. "Come on, Miranda, we have to go."

Miranda glared then turned to smile at Adeel. "Daddy sent me a red raincoat, but Aunt Sarah took it away."

Wow. The kid was still mad at her about that! The fight was fierce. Miranda actually walked up and kicked Sarah on the leg - the extent of her short reach.

Adeel backed away, a startled look.

Sarah gripped Miranda by the shoulders and bent, trying to keep her voice low, out of Adeel's earshot. "If you want to be a detective, you first have to be a good citizen. You can't let cookies get in the way or guide your life."

Miranda kicked again. Sarah grabbed one of the kid's flailing arms, holding tight, and hissed into her ear, "Listen, young lady, we're going home. Now! We have detective work to do. Unless you'd rather be wearing knee socks and white blouses dictated by Madame le Clerc, you'd better shape up. Darned quick."

The invocation of the late French nanny did the trick.

"Okay," Miranda said, with her trademark coy smile. "I'll be good."

"Ta, ta," Sarah waved two fingers in Adeel's direction, and off they went.

151

CHAPTER 36

Sarah was in a quandary. She had planned to go to Père Lachaise to look for Bernhardt's grave as soon as they left the Jardin des Plantes. She needed to keep channeling the great actress for help with the role of the old-lady psychic. They were going to rehearse at Gomez's place tonight, hoping police would soon finish their forensics at the theater. But she needed to tell Detective Vidal that Adeel had been in London the same time she was. She hated to use her mobile, she'd once again forgotten to charge it, and the call would no doubt take a while. Besides, it hardly seemed appropriate to be spouting clues while crammed in the metro.

She was walking with Miranda back to the Gare Austerlitz stop, pondering where to go next.

"You said we had to give information to the detective," Miranda's tone was insistent. "Let's go to the police station."

"He's probably busy right now," Sarah said. "We can call him from home. I think we should go look for Bernhardt's grave."

"The police station is more fun."

A kid pout was on its way, Sarah could feel it. "Detectives are never in their office. They question witnesses at the crime scene."

"Where's that?" Miranda demanded.

"Huh… Maybe the detective could meet us where we're going," Sarah hedged.

"I don't *want* to go to the cemetery. Daddy and I go there a lot to look at famous people."

"Don't forget that you and I found a clue at the other cemetery. Detective Vidal thinks the man in the bowtie at Baudelaire's grave is a suspect."

Miranda frowned. "I'm trying to remember."

"You know. The guy who quoted poetry. Something about the prince of clouds."

Miranda stopped and stared at her aunt with suspicion. "That was a clue?"

"Sure. That's what the detective said. If you're going to learn, you have to listen to the professionals."

"So, where are we going?" Miranda asked with resignation, her reluctance obvious.

Sarah's phone beeped. "Oh, a text from Mary wanting to know where we are. I'm telling her we're on our way to Bernhardt's grave."

As they approached the steps leading down to the labyrinth that had previously confused her, Sarah decided to stop and telephone. "Mary seems to have lots of questions."

"Big people always text in Paris. It costs too much to call," Miranda informed her aunt.

"If you don't mind, Miranda, I'm going to phone." Damn, the kid had to correct her about everything! Although it would suck down her battery. She'd taken too many pictures of Miranda on that weird giraffe.

Mary, of course, was concerned that Sarah couldn't find her way. "Don't worry," Sarah assured her, "I got directions.

John gave 'em to me after I fouled up that first time, when the librarian sent me to Baudelaire. That reminds me, I've got to return those borrowed books. But dread seeing her."

It went on from there. Did Sarah realize that Père Lachaise was huge, difficult to locate a specific grave? Maybe wait and go another time, it was getting late. Mary even suggested meeting them and going along.

"Mary, by time we wait to find you, it will be late," Sarah countered. "I'm just gonna make a quick run to the grave. I know how to get there."

She hung up, and off they went.

Sarah pulled out her phone again as she and Miranda came up from the Philippe Auguste metro. John's map was quite clear. She could see the short way to the cemetery from where they stood.

Mary was already there. After hearing Detective Vidal's concerns about Sarah and the child, she'd decided she had only one course — tail them! Should be easy enough to stay well behind and still keep them in sight in the immense expanse of the hilly burial ground with its infinite spread of gravestones and monuments. A fast call to John had instructed her which entrance he had provided on Sarah's map. "Good for you," he'd said, when Mary told him her plan. "If someone's stalking Sarah, and that is certainly what it sounds like, we should set up a relay team of watchers."

Mary had gotten to the Philippe Auguste stop quickly then stationed herself on the sidewalk behind the ubiquitous big map of the quarter. Easy enough to lean over the scrolled grillwork surrounding the wide stairs to the underground station and watch the comings and goings of commuters.

Sure enough, she heard Miranda's chatter before she could see them. Peeking around from her sign, she saw the kid's blonde curls rising, then the white Lady Gaga T-shirt so big it covered whatever she had underneath, and finally bright red sandals. Should be easy enough to keep track of that from a distance. Sarah's average height and jeans-clad legs and trainers would hardly stand out. If Sarah let the kid stray, which one would the stalker follow?

Mary almost laughed out loud at herself for jumping to the conclusion that some creep was out there with absolutely no evidence. She'd seen someone she thought she'd seen once before. Sarah, of course, now claimed four sightings. *On verra,* we shall see.

Aunt and child made their way across the metro island, crossed the street, passed by a corner bistro, and headed for a leafy walkway into the cemetery. Mary hung back. She could easily track them and certainly didn't want to risk being seen. As she paused in front of a shop window, she saw a guy wearing a cap with a fleur de lys logo come up the metro steps, take a quick look around, then head in the same direction as Sarah and Miranda. When he passed behind her, Mary turned from the window and snapped his picture.

CHAPTER 37

Sarah studied her map. It looked easy enough on paper, but surveying the vast tomb-filled expanse stretching out before her was daunting. Thanks be, John had printed it as well as put it on her phone. Her screen had gone completely black for lack of juice. Sarah Bernhardt, circled in red, seemed straight ahead, yet still a long walk. To her left was what appeared to be a large area of nobodies — except for Balzac — who, even so, were pretty far away.

"I told you the police station was more fun," Miranda said.

"I've got a picture of Bernhardt's grave," Sarah retorted. "I'm sure we'll recognize it when we see it." She handed her copy to Miranda. "Come on. It's a beautiful place. Like a park. According to the map, Chopin is off to the right. But let's move it. I have a rehearsal later."

Miranda trudged along, silently scuffing her sandals, kicking at bits of dirt or rock or whatever presented itself.

"There's one that looks like the picture," Miranda suddenly yelled, pointing off to a small rectangular thing crammed amid a jumble of gravesites and monuments.

"It looks like a doghouse," Sarah howled. "Under that

stupid little roof, it's even got an entrance for Fido. I'd imagined something grander. It's dwarfed by all this other stuff around."

With Sarah's rant, several nearby tourists, most snapping selfies (there were no apparent mourners in sight), turned, startled.

"That's it? That's all the Great One deserves?" Sarah continued her oration. "With all these monuments, that's all she gets? I can't believe it."

Miranda squinted at her aunt then shrugged.

Sarah grit her teeth and marched toward what she saw as a pathetic little crypt shaped liked a long gray box. Perhaps, if she reached out for it, she could touch Bernhardt's soul, the woman who so embraced death that from time to time she slept in a rosewood coffin. Sarah stopped, placed her hand on the cold granite.

"Upon such sacrifice," she cried, "the gods themselves throw incense. Howl, O! you men of stones: Had I your tongues and eyes, I'd use them so that heaven's vaults should crack. She's gone forever. Why should a dog, a horse, a rat, have life, and thou no breath at all? Thou'lt come no more. Undo this button."

"Gee, ma'am, is this some distant relative?" queried an American in a baseball cap who'd stopped to stare. "It seems to mean an awful lot to you."

"It's nobody. Just some old actress," Miranda said.

"Sure enough? These French cemeteries are for us tourists, just like those at home in New Orleans."

"We live here," Miranda said.

"Is that a fact?" The young man looked surprised. "You both sound like Americans."

"We are," Miranda said.

"Oh." The man beamed. "Maybe you know then how I can find Jim Morrison. That's the one I'm looking for."

"I'm going next to Moliere," Sarah said. "I hope he's been treated better than Bernhardt."

"Moliere?"

"He's an actor too."

"Don't say? Don't think I know him."

"Look at this great map," Sarah said. "You can find Morrison on here."

Mary watched, moving slowly, all the while clicking away with phone at eye, hiding her face, she hoped, in case Sarah or Miranda should glance back in her direction.

She caught what surely was the handing over of Sarah's map. The trio then moved on upward, barely stopping other than to shake a rock from a shoe. No peering at other gravestones or monuments. They clearly had a destination! What now had this obvious stalker in the ball cap talked the gullible Sarah into?

Was this bloke new? Had they seen him before? Mary tried to pull up a vision of the face under the deer stalker's hat. Certainly nothing memorable about the glimpse in the Orsay. Mary was torn about disengaging her camera long enough to phone John. But what would she say? Ask for guidance? Warn there was danger? Tell him to call the police? It seemed more imperative at the moment to keep track of them, keep a record.

And then they were gone! Sarah, Miranda, and the guy in the cap. The trio headed behind a row of close-together stone cabinets, and poof! Mary stuffed her phone in her pocket, quickened her pace. It was difficult to run. The terrain was hardly amenable to a chase.

CHAPTER 38

Mary arrived at John's out of breath and overwrought. "Sit down. Calm down. What is it?" John was frowning, Bisquit jumping. He led her into the salon.

"I lost them. And her phone just flips to answer."

"You found them at Pere Lachaise? Then lost them, Sarah and Miranda?"

"Yes!" Mary plopped down in a chair to catch her breath.

"It's getting late. Maybe Sarah took Miranda home," John said, reasonably. "Then went to work on that show."

Ben came in with drinks.

"I'll call," John said.

"No good," Mary retorted. "I told you, phone doesn't work."

"Yeah, Sarah never ever remembers to plug hers in." John pulled his cell from his pocket. "I even bought her a mobile charger, but she forgets that too. I'm dialing Vicki."

John brightened when Vicki answered.

"Everything fine," he silently mouthed over to Mary with a thumbs up gesture. He asked a few questions, continued to nod as he listened, waved Ben to hand him a drink.

Mary and Ben were on him the minute he hung up. "*Qu'est-ce que se* passé?" from Ben.

"What?" Mary demanded.

"Okay, okay." John, who had been pacing the room as he listened, sat down hard. "Miranda's home and fine, other than dirt and rocks in her shoes and a filthy Lady Gaga T-shirt. Vicki didn't sound upset. Said Miranda reported they fell down a mountain."

"A mountain?" Mary all but screeched.

"Vicki just laughed. Said any sort of slope is a mountain, as far as the kid is concerned."

"*Et Sarah?*" Ben asked.

"She handed Miranda over at the door, some guy behind her. Said she was late for rehearsal."

"Wearing a ball cap?" Mary demanded.

"Vicki didn't say."

"So much for tailing," Mary groaned. "No way anyone can keep up with her. I should call Vidal about this latest guy, but he'll kill me if I say I followed them."

"Mary, don't worry so," John said. "Sarah wouldn't have picked up with him, if he were the one she's seen four times before."

"Let's hope." She pulled out her phone. "I'll show you the pictures."

She had several clear shots.

"Doubt he's the one you've both seen before." John shook his head. "You said he was Brit. This one looks American."

"Why?"

"Clothes. The NFL cap."

Mary squinted at him. "The cap? It's got a fleur de lys."

John laughed. "Yeah. New Orleans. The New Orleans Saints. Most likely an American tourist. Sarah being friendly with a fellow traveler."

CHAPTER 39

Sarah buzzed herself into Gomez's building. Late, again. She really pressed herself too thin. Babysitter, sleuth. Wasn't leaving enough time for work.

The director, of course, was angry. "Late, every time late. Vhen vill you fix?"

"Sorry. But I assumed you'd be rehearsing Margery in her new role."

"So, you now ze director?"

Sommes piped up. "The good news, ta da. We're back in the theater tomorrow. The police gave us an okay."

"Yes. Tomorrow morning, early. So ve can rehearse Miss Star here," Gomez gestured at Sarah, "before she has to leave for nanny-sitting job. Now ve haf urgency. Ve haf one week. The producers demand. Then ve must open for business."

Sarah threw herself into the mindset of being elderly and blind. Her performance was inspired. After she'd touched the great one's grave, Bernhardt was on her shoulders — in her limp, her face, her voice. Even Gomez was awed. "Bravo," he said, as he called it a night.

Sommes suggested that the cast retreat to a nearby bistro for a drink.

"Swell idea," Sarah replied. "I could use a sandwich, haven't eaten since breakfast."

As soon as they were settled with a large carafe, her *croque monsieur* on the way, Sarah began asking questions of the Londoners. Had any of them worked with Georgie before? Did they know her ex-husband? Had they seen The Scottish Play that she and Sarah had done together?

"The police asked us all this," Sommes grumped. "Who are you now, Miss Marple?"

Rachel, always the peacemaker, waved her hand, as though clearing smoke. "She's quite right. We are an ensemble. We may well have some knowledge that could shed light on this. I, for one, knew Georgie by reputation. She worked in London theater for years. And you, Mr. Sommes?"

"Well, in point of fact, perhaps I did see that production of The Scottish Play. I certainly remember reading about it." He stopped and lifted his chin toward Sarah. "Although, surely, if I'd witnessed your sterling performance, it would be seared in my memory."

"And you Paul? Margery?" Rachel continued, brushing past Sommes and his snide remark.

They were on their second carafe by time the reminiscences had finished and Sarah was able to say, wiping sticky ham and cheese from her fingers, "Okay, here are the highlights of my notes for Detective Vidal. Wow. Some of this is really interesting!

"Number one item: Paul thinks he remembers Ann-Sophie from a fringe production a year or so ago. In London. She, the so-called non-English speaker!"

"I said, perhaps." Paul interjected. "It's a fleeting memory of someone in wardrobe. But I think I mentioned it to the detective when he quizzed us after her murder."

"Yes," Sarah said gleefully. "I suspect that you did. Because when the good detective got around to questioning me, he was asking about London more than the death of Ann-Sophie, our so-called seamstress. I was surprised at the time.

"Okay, item number two: Sommes seems to remember reading about a change in the lead role of The Scottish Play well before the production was mounted. No idea what the switch was about or where he read it, but we should search for the item. Marjery thinks she remembers the same story. Again, no idea where.

"Item three: Rachel did a show several years ago in which an older actor was dismissed the first day of rehearsal for drugs, and rumor was he was Georgie's husband. Like my memory of someone who was said to have been Georgie's ex, just last year, being dismissed from The Scottish Play.

"Finally, item number four: This doesn't seem to have anything to do with us now. But Rachel worked with Blane Gowan, the first dead actress in the psychic role, who turned out to have a side job as an MI6 spy. She was an accomplished performer, good reputation. But she did take a lot of sick days. Understudies loved her. Interesting because Sommes has kept thinking there's a spy agency connection with the latest murders. But none of us can sort out how."

"Well," sniped Sommes, "Miss Marple lives. Or, better yet, Mademoiselle, le Sleuth." He smiled at Sarah. "No offense, this was probably an excellent idea. I'm sure these French coppers know nothing about English theater."

They all prepared to leave when Sommes frowned. "Hang on," he said, snapping his fingers. "Are any of you familiar with a spot behind Gare Montparnasse with a strip of theaters called Gaité Street. Strange place. A bit of everything, as near as I could tell. Burlesque, French plays, Italian. Went with an acquaintance the other night to see an English one. Dreadful piece with a bloke who seemed somewhat familiar. Classically trained actor in a simply unintelligible play. Wondered how such a guy would stoop so low."

"So, could this be Georgie's husband?" Sarah asked. "Here. And desperate for work."

"Honestly can't say why it came to mind. Just an association with down and out actors. My friend said he met up with this fellow once and that he was a bit of a nutter. Thought rather well of himself but was a nobody really. Obsessed with Princess Diana."

CHAPTER 40

Mary was sitting, drink in hand, in John's living room when Sarah opened the front door. "You're all right!" she exclaimed. John had gone to the kitchen to rustle another bottle of wine.

"Of course," Sarah looked startled. "Why not?"

"Where did you go?"

"The cemetery, I told you that. Then rehearsal …"

"No, I …" Mary faltered. Gad. She couldn't admit she'd been sneaking around following them.

John yelled from the kitchen, "You're home. I'll bring another glass."

Mary needn't have worried about covering her tracks. Sarah launched right in. "What a day! I got the most wonderful inspiration from Bernhardt's tomb. Her spirit soared through me. And I have tons of clues for your detective."

"He's not MY detective." Mary's response was knee-jerk. Why did she keep doing that?

"Who's NOT your detective?" John joined them carrying a bottle and another glass along with cheese and bread. "I hate to be like Sarah and keep falling back on the Bard, but 'the lady doth…'"

"That's enough," Mary said. "A fair observation. I've made note of it myself."

"After Bernhardt, we went to Moliere. It's too bad you weren't with us Mary, (at this Mary shot a pleading look at John) it was amazing," Sarah went on. "They had to bury him at night because he was an actor. The indignity. Can you imagine!"

John sprouted a wide grin, but inclined his head to Mary ever so slightly in an answering yes. "What's this about Moliere?" he asked Sarah.

"He now has a proper monument, with a fence around it and flowers. Not like poor Bernhardt, or Jim Morrison, for that matter. He has a puny site as well."

"No night burials for them, huh?"

"Of course not. Moliere was way before when they still had a horrid law that actors couldn't be buried in sacred ground."

"All very interesting," Mary said slowly, "but what else did you do?"

"Went to rehearsal. I was already late."

"Why late?"

"Busy day!" Sarah looked at Mary like she was stupid. "You know, all the stuff crammed in. The Orsay, the skeleton museum. And that's where I got a clue for," Sarah gave her a sly nod, "the detective who isn't yours."

Mary closed her eyes and took a deep breath. "Go on."

"Adeel," Sarah said gleefully. "You remember Adeel from the mosque."

Mary exhaled softly. "Afraid not." Then inspiration hit. She waited a beat. "Oh, was he at the cemetery with you?"

"No," Sarah said dismissively, "that was Jimmy John from

New Orleans. Well, anyway," Sarah went on, "the detective who isn't yours knows about Adeel. And I found out that he was in London the same time I did Lady Macbeth there. AND — drum roll, please – we, the cast, I mean, think Ann-Sophie was, as well! That murdered seamstress who claimed she couldn't speak English."

"Hmm," John said. "That does sound like news. You've got Vidal's number? I'd call him first thing tomorrow." He paused. "Unless Mary wants to, of course."

"Great idea!" Sarah laughed, as Mary's color rose, moving up her neck nearly reaching her ears.

"So anyway," Sarah moved on without a stop for breath, "what do you guys know about Gaité Street?"

"Never heard of it." Mary's response was quick, eager to move away from both Vidal and the guy with the New Orleans cap.

"Ah, some sort of semi-red-light district, I think. Over near Gare Montparnasse." John shook his head. "Where did you come up with that?"

CHAPTER 41

When Sarah called early the next day to give Vidal her new information, he insisted upon coming to talk rather than taking it over the phone. Turned out, as Sarah had guessed, that he already knew about Ann-Sophie's time in London. Adeel's as well.

"We Paris police are thorough, Mademoiselle," he said. "But please to understand, we are grateful for *l'information*. Is always excellent to cooperate with authorities." He set his cup down squarely.

She was surprised he'd accepted coffee and was much more relaxed than the last time he'd been here when he asked about her London robbery and stolen poetry book. Now it felt like he wanted to chat.

"And so, what else can you tell me of the man with the battered briefcase seen among the trees. Clothes he wore? A tie? Did he have a hat?"

"I honestly think it wasn't Adeel. But I couldn't swear to it. I feel fairly certain that the guy who bumped us on the stairs was the same person I later spotted among the trees. And I wondered the moment I saw Adeel at the carousel if that was him again. But I doubted it even then. The thing that seemed important was that his time in London coincided with mine."

"Quite so."

Sarah frowned. "How did you know about Ann-Sophie being there as well?"

"Her mother said she lived in London. They speak not for a year."

"Wow!" Sarah exclaimed. "Working in our show and pretending she didn't speak English! I knew she was faking. But wow!"

Vidal smiled.

"So, Detective, we need to find out who in the cast knew her. How she got that job. Right?"

Vidal nodded.

Sarah smiled sheepishly. "Alas. I have the dullness of a fool."

Excitement reigned. The yellow crime tape was gone. They were back in the little theater behind the disco. No new wardrobe mistress was in residence this morning because the actors were in the same roles. Their costumes fit. Sarah had yet to speak her first line, but she'd already asked each and every one of cast and crew how Ann-Sophie had gotten her job here. No one knew!

"Okay. Places," Gomez yelled. Everyone stepped into his or her assigned spot, and the play began.

"Don't look now," Margery-as-Laura says to her husband, "but those two Englishwomen over there have been studying us since we came in."

Sommes-as-John: "Oh, for god's sake, Laura, can we give it a miss, for once?"

Sarah, thanks to her encounter with Bernhardt the day before in Père Lachaise cemetery, pushed the mystery of Ann-Sophie from her mind and became old, blind, psychic, and British.

CHAPTER 42

Rehearsal over, Sarah had to rush away to pick up Miranda at school. Scurrying past shoppers on the street of the Old Temple toward her metro stop, she pondered what to do next, who to question. Gomez should be the key. How could he not know how Ann-Sophie suddenly appeared and began tucking and pinning? But he'd shrugged, looked surprised when Sarah quizzed him after she first arrived at the theater this morning. His only response had been, "Zoes pushy producers, zay into everyzing."

Shoving into a metro car with all the other weary commuters, Sarah was able to grab a jump seat by the door. She reveled in her success at learning these mass-transit moves. London and Paris were certainly a far cry from the car-driven existence of California!

She settled in and returned to wondering about Gomez saying he didn't know how Ann-Sophie was hired. The guy was weird. Hard to figure his deal. Always laying every problem to shadowy producers. Sarah sat up straighter. Of course. They had no stage manager! That heavy-set, pimply faced girl had quit after the first two murders. Things had been so muddled and chaotic since — with no proper rehearsals or much of anything coherent — was it possible that Ann-Sophie just stepped in and started working and no one noticed?

But wow — that was fast becoming her favorite word. Someone had to have done a lot of planning to murder Georgie in the dressing room, come on stage with her cane, then walk off to garrote the stagehand. And, after that, install Ann-Sophie as a seamstress before doing her in with her own scissors. Wow, indeed.

Sarah was at her usual spot leaning against the metal rails outside the sand-colored building with the French flag when Miranda came bounding out with her loaded school satchel waving her latest drawing. "I did the Dodo carousel, see."

"That's great. There's the giraffe and the turtle. What a good job. And what's this pink thing off to the side?"

"The cake Adeel promised when we go again."

"What? I didn't hear that."

"Yes. You made us leave too early. He promised cakes next time. Is it today?"

Sarah forced a smile. "Ah, no, little kiddo, we can get cookies someplace else. I think there's some of those yummy chocolate ones mommy bakes at home."

"I want to go with Adeel. He's nice, and I like the cushions at the mosque."

"Maybe we'll all go to the mosque when daddy gets back."

"No. He's always away. I like Adeel. He's nice."

"Miranda," Sarah could hear herself almost yelling. What the devil could she do or say now? Clearly dangerous territory. "Miranda," she took a deep breath and started again, "we have to pay attention to Detective Vidal, if we want to be detectives. He said to be careful about who we talk to.

"Say, I have an idea! There's a fun place sort of near here, I think, called Gaité Street. We could go there and look for cotton candy or something."

"What's fun about it?" Miranda asked.

They came up from the Gaité metro stop, and the first thing Sarah spotted was a large storefront that identified itself as *l'Odyssex*. *Oh boy*, she thought, *that's not hard to translate.*

"Maybe we should go home," she said squeezing tighter on Miranda's hand.

"No, let's look for cotton candy."

"Sorry, Babe, I've put us in the wrong place. I must have misread the map."

She looked down the short block and could see theater signs, hotels, ordinary restaurants. "Well, it might be okay. Let's just walk to the end of this block."

"Why did you say cotton candy if they don't have it?"

"I thought it was like a circus or something. I misunderstood."

Sarah steeled herself and breathed a sigh of relief as she distracted her niece by pointing at the blue façade of *La Comédie Italienne* across the street while she scooted them past the storefront of *l'Odyssex* with its sign for "*salons et cabines grand luxe.*"

They went past a music hall, a couple of theaters, several restaurants including Thai and Japanese, a three-star hotel then suddenly another erotic shop. To Sarah's horror, its façade advertised "sex toys." They were right there, before she spotted it. John was right. It was something of a red-light district. Miranda skipped past without a glance, pulling at Sarah's hand, obviously hoping to find cotton candy.

Gosh, Sarah thought, maybe the kid doesn't read well in English since she's in French school all day. But that's ridiculous. She has all sorts of books at home. Hard to believe she doesn't know or just didn't see the word "toy." Another escape! She had to find a different metro stop. She didn't want to backtrack past the sex shops again.

Finally, near the end of the block, Sarah spotted Montparnasse Theater, a large building standing out from the rest with an entrance on its side to a smaller venue. A wall poster said its offering was in English. "Here it is," she exclaimed.

"There's nothing here," Miranda said. "Not even hotdogs or popcorn."

"No, I mean the show Sommes was talking about."

Sarah peered at promos on the side of the building and saw publicity photos of a middle-years man with slicked-back, black hair, identified as James Powell. Certainly wasn't the handsome gray-haired man at Georgie's casket viewing. So much for that theory!

Then suddenly with no sense of where he came from, slicked-back hair was at her side.

"Good day, Mademoiselle." A British accent, no hat.

Sarah tried to visualize him with a mustache, a beret, a bowler, a deerstalker cap. She wished he were anyone but this guy, even the drug-dreamy gray-haired guy. *Anyone* but this smiler with no hat. She felt a chill on the warm day.

"Diana," he said, moving in so close, Sarah and Miranda were forced closer to the wall. She put her hand out to the publicity poster to push back from falling into it. "My lovely Diana."

"Her name's not Diana," shouted Miranda, her voice muffled as it echoed across the barrier wall.

Sarah felt pinned in. The guy was breathing down her neck. How to break away? She squeezed Miranda's hand then moved up a bit to grab her wrist.

The kid used the motion to swivel on the guy, kick him in the shin, then take Sarah's hand, and the two took off running to laughter at their backs.

CHAPTER 43

Sarah finally got back to John's, exhausted. He was warming her dinner in the microwave.

"They keep piling up, problems," she announced as she flopped onto one of the high stools at the round kitchen table. "This stalker, the Man in Disguise. And Adeel, Miranda's going to keep at it. He promises her cakes and she's hooked. Wants to keep meeting him."

"What's this about a stalker?"

"At that red-light district, you mentioned. Should never have gone." She filled him in on what had just happened.

"The guy didn't touch you. Didn't say anything but call you Diana? Maybe he mistook you for someone else," John replied.

"I'm telling you, he's the guy who keeps turning up everywhere. He's following me."

"But you just said his picture was there. He was in the play. He thought you were a fan, staring at his poster."

"We were scared. Miranda kicked him."

John set a plate of pasta in front of her. "Parmesan?" He held out a grater and small piece of cheese.

"We're opening in a week. This role is so demanding. My

hardest ever. I don't know how women can be mothers and have a career too."

"Way beyond me. It's all I can do to keep my business running and take care of this apartment. So? Cheese or no?"

Sarah nodded yes. "Few people live on the lovely scale you do. And you're a perfectionist. But what am I to do? Miranda will insist on going back for cakes. And Adeel's a suspect."

John grated Parmesan, shrugged and shook his head.

"It's a wise parent who knows her own child. Miranda will insist on those cakes. But, poor baby, if I give up, she'll be back stuck with Madame le Clerc."

"I wish I could help." John's tone, as always, was sympathetic. "But if I brought her into the shop, she'd have the place in chaos in no time. Why not ask Vidal? Maybe set up some sort of sting-meeting with Adeel. Watch what happens."

"Use Miranda as a pawn? Never!"

CHAPTER 44

Next day, before going to rehearsal, Sarah made a call to London. "Felicity? Hi. Sarah Donohue here. We spoke a few weeks ago about the Paris production of *Don't Look Now*."

"Oh my, yes." Sarah could hear the gasp through the agent's lockjaw drawl. "More murders since. What IS going on over there? I would never send a client."

Sarah grinned. A perfect opening for her main questions. No sense in asking about Ann-Sophie, since Felicity was an actor's agent and wouldn't know anything about a seamstress. "I suppose Director Gomez has approached you for help in finding someone?"

"Quite. He's begged every agency in the city."

"Yes. He desperately needs an old woman. I'm doing the role until he finds someone closer to the proper age."

"You?" The catching of breath was audible. "I do remember sending you for the Lady Macbeth audition a year or so ago. Almost against my better judgment, thinking you were too young even for that."

"My reviews were good."

"Quite. I was pleased."

"I know you represented Blane Gowan, the actress

murdered last month who turned out to be an MI6 spy. Did you represent Georgie and her ex-husband as well?"

"Quite. But I had to drop him. Drugs and alcohol."

"Yes. That's what we all thought. And was it him or another actor who was dropped from that Macbeth production I was in? Even before rehearsals began?"

"The Paris police have asked me about all of that. Perhaps you should speak with them. Lovely to talk, my dear. Give me a call if you're in the city again and need representation. I understand you were cast this time by someone in Los Angeles."

"Oh, yes." Sarah was panicky she was going to lose her before she got to the vital topic. "That was set up by the producers. Embarrassing. The ones Gomez keeps calling shady. Ian Sommes, I'm sure you know him, keeps insisting that they are somehow connected to the British spy bunch."

Felicity's laugh bordered on a snort. "Anything's possible. I was certainly taken in by that Blane Gowan/Jane Forsyth, whatever her name was. She was a fine actress but took a lot of sick days. Word is, though, that these moneymen Gomez is dealing with are exactly that — all money and no brains. Los Angeles real estate barons with theatrical pretensions. They want to outdo their Beverley Hills neighbors who roll the dice at backing films."

"Oh," was all Sarah could muster. But she was delighted with that info. No spies, just amateur angels.

"I must ring off. Good luck. It sounds like you'll need it."

CHAPTER 45

Sarah gripped Miranda's hand tightly as they walked toward the Dodo Carousel. Miranda skipped and tried to shake loose the iron grip. Adeel, big grin in place, stood off to the right of a giant ostrich.

Sarah gasped with relief that he held no battered briefcase, only a large Printemps shopping bag. She was a wreck, worried about all the things that could go wrong. So what if Detective Vidal and his cops were swarming through the trees, that John and Ben were strategically situated?

It hadn't done much good to resist. Vidal had insisted this was a safe plan after John insisted on Sarah telling the detective about Ann-Sophie's mysterious hiring. "We have not a clue who is a *bon* suspect. Adeel seems as possible as anyone because he was in London same time as you and Ann-Sophie. And he just happens to meet you by hazard in *le jardin*? I think not."

Vidal purposely chose the dinner hour for the suggested rendezvous and alerted park officials to keep the Dodo ride open late. "We can not to worry that other children will be there." He was right. No kids, and the silence was eerie. The sun was not down but low and played with shadows among the trees. John and Ben had driven them to the nearby bus park along the river, but from there Sarah and Miranda had made their own way along the lush overhanging path through the *jardin*. Wise heads had decided that their two friends must stay out of sight for fear Miranda would spot them and give the game away.

Adeel approached. "I'm so pleased to see you. Should we take a ride on the carousel, Young Miss, before we go for cakes?"

"Yes." Miranda again tried to extricate herself from the iron grip, but Sarah couldn't let go. The adults had gone over this. She must allow the child to ride. But her muscles refused to obey.

Adeel looked perplexed. "Perhaps a drink of lemonade before we ride." He waved an arm at a tiny shack alongside, although it didn't appear to be open.

Sarah shook her head. She certainly didn't want to give him a chance to spike their drinks with knockout drops. She flexed her fingers, trying to get the blood circulating. She glanced down, and both she and the kid had digits that had turned bloodless white!

Miranda shook her arm hard, stared quizzically at her. Sarah let go. "Okay," she said.

Adeel was quickly at their side, took Miranda's hand, and the two bounded off to jump on the carousel. Sarah was right behind.

"Only the giraffes go up and down," he said. "Would you prefer that or a stationary animal?"

"You certainly are familiar with this children's ride," Sarah sniped.

"Oh, yes," he replied brightly. "I bring my nieces and nephews."

He lifted Miranda into the saddle of an ancient yellow giraffe with brown spots and black horns sticking straight up. The music started, and she was off shouting "giddy up."

Sarah swiveled frantically around, hoping to spot the reassuring presence of swarms of police, but saw no one. What if they weren't here? What if they had the day or the time mixed up? She hadn't seen a single human since Ben and John had dropped them off and then gone to park the car. What if they'd had an accident pulling into a parking space? What if Detective Vidal was called off to a fresh murder? What if? What if? *Oh my god*, she should never have agreed to this. Miranda came into view, kicking her little heels against the spotted giraffe yelling "giddy up, giddy up," and the ride moved on. But where was Adeel? He didn't seem to be anywhere on the carousel.

Next swing around, Sarah could hear the "giddy up," before Miranda came into view. But what a view it was. She was wearing a red mackintosh!

CHAPTER 46

Sarah could hear herself screaming as she ran toward Miranda, whose face blurred in and out, up and down on the painted giraffe. A whistle cut through the calliope sounds, and police swarmed from surrounding trees.

She scraped her knee scrambling aboard the circling carousel. As she tried to stand, the squawky music stopped, the merry-go-round came to an abrupt halt, and Sarah was thrown back to the floor.

Miranda, wrapped in red, grinned down from high astride her steed, halted in upward leap at its top ratchet. "*Les flics* are here."

And so they were. Uniforms lifted the child down from her perch and Sarah up from her fall. Then Adeel came into view, his arms cuffed behind.

Miranda, her slicker flapping, ran to him. "Monsieur Adeel."

Sarah screamed, "Get that horrid thing off her. Where did it come from?"

Vidal stepped in. "Indeed, monsieur, can you respond to that?"

"I don't understand." Adeel blinked, looked bewildered.

"It seems a simple question," Vidal snapped. "Where did the red rain hood come from?"

"Printemps," Adeel replied, the eye tics picking up speed.

"Not where did you buy?" Vidal snapped again. "More exactly, *pour quoi*? Why do you bedevil this family with such a thing?"

"Bedevil? I don't understand. The child asked for it."

"Asked for?" Sarah sputtered. "Ridiculous."

"And do you know the small theater off rue Vieille du Temple?" Vidal demanded.

"What?" Adeel said. "I don't understand."

"I regret, monsieur," Vidal said, "we must escort you to the Commissariat for further questions."

In an aside to Sarah, "We must speak with the young mademoiselle as well."

"Not now." What a nightmare. Vicki would kill her. She'd be late for rehearsal. And what a shock about Adeel. "I've got to get her back. Her mother will be home soon."

"Perhaps tomorrow would be a good time?" And Adeel was marched off in handcuffs.

CHAPTER 47

The scene at school was not pretty. Miranda stomped up to the waiting Sarah and kicked at her. "You're horrible. I lost another mackintosh. And Monsieur Adeel is in the slammer."

"Such language!" Sarah sputtered. "Too much TV."

"I hate you. You keep taking my present from Daddy."

"Your father did not send it. Adeel said he bought it at Printemps."

"He wanted me to have it. Not mean like you. Let's go get him sprung."

Sarah couldn't contain her laughter. "Miranda, you're impossible."

"It's not funny. He's in jail because of you."

"Sweetie, please be reasonable. He's dangerous."

"No! He's nice. Not like you."

Sarah had had a tough rehearsal, the show was to open in two days. And now this hurtful outburst! How could she keep up this pace? Adeel and his offer of cakes at the mosque had played havoc with everyone's life. But maybe the kid had a point. Adeel hardly seemed like a killer.

"Miranda, you're going to have to ease up, or I'll tell your mother to get Madame le Clerc back. I'm really under the gun with this play opening."

"What gun? You don't have a gun. And neither does Adeel."

Sarah laughed again. "Just an expression, baby."

Miranda stamped her foot. "I'm not a baby. I'm going to the jail to tell Adeel I'm sorry."

"That's absurd. We're not going to any jail!"

CHAPTER 48

Miranda had won again. Anything to shut the kid up. Mary had been enlisted to show Sarah and Miranda where Vidal "worked" so the three of them were off. Sarah had persuaded Mary with the reasoning that since Vidal wanted to quiz Miranda about how she had once again ended up wearing a red mackintosh, they could use that as an excuse for "visiting" the police.

As they entered the station house behind the Gare de l'Est, Mary shivered with her sense of *déjà vu*. Hard to believe it had been only a few weeks since she'd first come here to report her stolen handbag. How many murders ago was that? Six? All of this triggered because Miranda wouldn't allow her nanny to pack her rolly bag for a weekend trip to Prague!

Sure enough, there was the intransigent gatekeeper cop behind the big desk, listening to woes and shouting "*calmez vous*" to victims and criminals alike.

This was a ridiculous errand, and Mary wouldn't at all blame the pudgy *flic* for sneering at her mission. But she'd taken the precaution of calling Detective Vidal and setting up an appointment. It hadn't required much to convince him that indulging Miranda's fantasy of injecting herself into the process might pay off. The police had been cautious all along about questioning the child's recollection of events. Not only because of Vicki's fear of having her frightened, but clearly the investigators worried the kid might imagine details about how she came to possess the red mackintosh. On three separate occasions, so far! Mary shuddered at the thought of "so far." Would this nightmare never end?

The desk cop registered a flicker of recognition as Mary stepped up, but thankfully he didn't say "not you again."

"I have an appointment with Detective Vidal."

He nodded, pointed at a bench, said "Wait," and turned to his ringing phone.

CHAPTER 49

Miranda was so excited her Mary Janes barely touched the ground as she waved goodbye to the fleshy officer behind the big desk.

"I sprung him, I sprung him. I told you I would," she all but shouted.

How could one so young manage gleeful and smug at the same time, Mary wondered.

Sarah, doing well with both smug and glee herself, retorted, "I told you, if you dressed properly and didn't wear Lady Gaga, the detective would take your testimony seriously."

"Okay, but I'm taking this stupid bow out right now." She reached to her hair and snatched the offending satin bauble, which Sarah grabbed and stuck in her handbag.

"No one to spring," Mary's exasperation was running over. "Adeel was gone when we got there. You heard Detective Vidal."

They were out on the sidewalk by now, in front of the commissariat with its ugly white stone front.

"He said I was a good detective." Miranda was now doing a haughty that was quite impressive for a four-year-old. "I told him the Cookie Man didn't do anything wrong. He bought me a mackintosh for the one from Daddy that the police took away."

"Adeel was gone by time we got there," Mary snapped. "They didn't have enough evidence."

Sarah glared, and Miranda got prissy, "I had the evidence. I'm the detective, not you."

"My mistake," Mary said, grinding her teeth, yet chastising herself for forgetting that adults ought not interfere with a child's fantasy. "So where do we go from here?"

"On the subject of sleuthing," Sarah said, "I need to do some research to find an item from London theatrical trade papers last year. Two separate cast members think they read that someone got dismissed from The Scottish Play before I was cast."

"Hmm," Mary said. "What's that about?"

" I just wonder — have a hunch — he could be the stalker, the Master of Disguise. If I can find the item, I'd have his name and could check out my suspicion that the jerk who scared us at that theater is the same guy."

"I'm going to search too," Miranda said. "I'm a good detective."

"The elusive bloke! That would be a find," Mary replied. "*Allons-y!*"

CHAPTER 50

Sarah and a strutting Miranda took leave from Mary at her metro line. The kid talked the rest of the way about what a good detective she was. "I told you I would get Adeel sprung," she said to Sarah at least five times.

As they climbed the stairs at their St. Francis stop, Miranda announced, "I've got to tell Ninon I solved a crime. She's just a little kid so she probably won't understand. But I want to tell her." Miranda was, indeed, about six months older than Ninon and in a different level at the *maternelle*. But her level of sophistication and street smarts, if you will, was light-years away from not just the fragile-looking and timid Ninon but from the bulk of their contemporaries as well.

Trying to head off more commotion, Sarah said, "Telling Ninon will be a fun thing at school tomorrow."

"No," Miranda said. "Her house is over there. I want to tell her now."

"It's close to dinner time. And we have to walk Chess," Sarah countered.

"That's fine. Chess likes Ninon, too."

Sarah shrugged. She was too weary to argue. Miranda

was bursting with the mistaken notion that lack of evidence against Adeel boiled down to her having engineered his release.

They hurried home, leashed up Chess, then headed for the trickier task of getting permission to take Ninon for a run in the park. Her reluctant mother remembered only too well that the last time Sarah was in charge of the girls they were hauled off by gangsters while the police gave chase. Now the two children pleaded in unison for Ninon to be allowed to go play.

"S'il te plait, s'il te plait, Maman. Si vous plait, s'il vous plait, Madame Boisseau." The besieged mother gave in and said, "Okay."

Well, at least something translates, Sarah thought.

She and the two children headed to the green space that divided the street in front of Vicki's apartment, Chess leading the way at an expectant trot, Miranda dancing behind gripping the leash. When they hit the lawn, the girls began rough-housing with the dog while Sarah settled in at a bench to begin her phone search for the probably two-year-old trade item about an actor being dropped from The Scottish Play before she, Sarah, joined the cast.

Frustrating search. Amazing how many were axed from productions before a show got up. Must be something telling there — were that many actors taking drugs? Or did directors just keep changing their minds? Or agents sending out the wrong people on calls?

Sarah glanced up at the girls and Chess, all three running in circles around the indentation surrounding a non-working fountain. She sighed with relief. Thank heaven, no water spouting. That's all she'd need, to have to present Ninon's mom with a soaking-wet child. She bent back to her research and noted something about a Scottish Play production with a date shortly before Sarah joined the cast. As she excitedly scrolled toward the item, Miranda's voice shot through her consciousness. The kid was yelling.

Sarah's head jerked up from her phone. Chess was barking, Miranda screaming, "*Allez, allez!*" and throwing handfuls of gravel at someone in a yellow polka-dot shirt retreating across the grass.

"What happened? What?" Sarah was shouting as she sprinted the short distance.

"That guy was trying to give us candy," Miranda said with a self-satisfied smug. "Ninon was about to take it. She's just a little kid. She doesn't know any better."

"Smart Big Girl." Sarah grabbed her niece in a bear hug.

CHAPTER 51

Sarah hurried, late as usual, up the narrow alleyway alongside the old rabbinical store turned disco. Again, another opening night. She was terrified. Not sure which was worse — fear of being murdered by critics or just plain murdered. She must cling to her image of Bernhardt who had played a nineteen-year-old when she was sixty-five. Sarah had to do it in reverse: play a seventy-four-year-old at twenty-six.

She opened the stage door to the usual chaos, actors at high pitch, crew bumping around moving sets. Pierre greeted her with a reassuring grin and a kiss on both cheeks. She could hear Gomez yelling somewhere off to her left. Headlong down the spiral staircase, she stopped short in the dressing room door: another vase, actually more like an urn, but no flowers! No one around. Lights ablaze circling the dressing table mirror where Georgie was stabbed to death.

Sarah steeled herself and approached cautiously. She peered into the darkness of the urn. No water for missing flowers, but something. What? She pulled out her cell, shining its light into the interior. Sand perhaps? As she bent closer, a waft of smoke. Ashes! Her heart thumped. What was this? It couldn't be a burial urn, it had no lid. She ran a trembling hand around its rough surface, found a white envelope with card. Neatly printed block letters in red ink:

Oh, London is a man's town, there's power in the air,
And Paris is a woman's town, with flowers in her hair
So it's home again, home again, America for me.
My heart is turning home again, and there I long to be.

Sarah's heart skipped. Why was this familiar? "Home again?"

The graffiti after the London robbery! "Go Back to America." But that wasn't exactly it.

Of course! That was the poem John had found. And what did the poet have to do with the robbery? Her mind was shut down. Damn it. She couldn't seem to remember anything except that she had to get into her costume and onto the stage.

She aimed her cell, clicked on urn and poem then, fingers shaking, dialed John.

"More flowers," she whispered, looking again around the dressing room. The others must be costumed and upstairs, ready to begin. And she was late! She raised her voice above the whisper. "Not really flowers, an urn — I think it's ashes — poem about flowers. What do I do?"

"Call the police," John instructed, but Sarah scotched that.

"We've got to put this play on TONIGHT, or it will never get up. Swarming police would wreck it."

"Then why did you ask for advice?" His impatience came through loud and clear.

"Because I don't know what to do," she wailed.

"I have to go," she went on in a rush. "I shouldn't have touched the envelope. They'll find fingerprints, won't they, even with mine there?

"Oh my god," she said as she spotted an unfamiliar poster taped to a back wall.

"What is it?" John's voice boomed from the phone that in her agitation she'd slammed down on a counter.

"A woman lying in cathedral rubble. It's tumbling down."

"Sarah, make sense." John's voice again. "Pick up the phone."

She put it to her ear. "There's a huge poster that wasn't here. A woman in distress. Her hand up in supplication to ward off the falling debris."

"Take a picture," John yelled. "I'm heading into the theater now."

Just as Sarah hit her send button, Rachel arrived to admonish her to get upstairs. "Gomez is apoplectic."

"Did you put that up?" Sarah asked, waving her hand at the poster.

"Heavens, no, never saw it." Rachel's eyes widened. "How offensive. The church crumbling down around her."

"Who could have done this?" Sarah moaned.

"Speaking of 'never saw,'" Rachel said, "some bloke with stringy hair held the stage door for me when I entered. Acted like he belonged here."

"Maybe the new prop man?" Sarah ventured with a sliver of hope, quickly eclipsed by better sense. More likely the guy with the urn.

Gomez's shouting came through the closed door. "On stage. Places."

Sarah quickly changed into her costume, picked up her tape, her dark glasses and headed for the stairs.

The auditorium was beginning to fill up. "This is *deja-vu*, if I've ever seen it," Mary quipped. "We friends of Sarah assemble once again."

"I'm her niece, and mommy is her sister," Miranda

corrected. "The rest of you are friends except for Monsieur Vidal. He's police."

"Thanks, Short Stuff, for clearing that up."

Another long night, Mary thought. Vicki's a dear friend, but the emoting sister and the smart-mouthed child can be taxing. She leaned toward John to grouse over the kid's antics, but realized to her surprise he and Ben had moved into the aisle and were engaged in animated conversation with Vidal. In fact, it seemed that Ben, uncharacteristically, was doing most of the talking.

They finally took their seats, lined up as they had two weeks before: Vidal, Mary, Miranda, Vicki. With John and Ben a row in front.

"What's up?" Mary asked the detective as soon as they were seated, but he shushed her as the curtain rose.

The stage was set as before. But instead of Sarah seated front with the actor Mary knew as Sommes, there was a sweet young thing she didn't know. This must be the Margery who was taking Sarah's role as the bereaved mother. At the back bistro table, along with an older woman, was Sarah, looking very much the elderly blind woman she was playing. Dark glasses and cane of course helped.

But to Mary's amazement, everything about the young California girl, even just sitting before she had uttered a word — posture, body movement, facial expression — *everything* told you this was an old lady who couldn't see! Mary remembered back to that first time she'd watched Sarah on stage at a rehearsal and how stunned she'd been at her transformation. Once again, she realized that this young woman truly had talent.

The play began, and with the first line, Miranda let out a

yelp, "That's him! That's him!" Mary saw that the kid was out of her seat and struggling with her mother, who was trying to control her. On stage, Sommes raised his voice in an effort to drown out the commotion. "Can't we . . ."

Vidal, next to Mary and fortunately on the aisle, looked over at Miranda and bounded from his seat. But instead of heading for the kid and slapping her silly, which Mary felt he should do, he was running toward the stage where Miranda kept pointing and yelling, "That's him! That's him!"

Mary swiveled back from the screaming child and saw a stringy-haired man in bright yellow start up the stage steps. The actors were on their feet by now, canes and dark glasses be damned. A bistro table turned over. Police seemed to come out of the woodwork. House lights went up, the curtain fell, just as the unkempt guy, a blade glistening in his hand, escaped under its folds.

CHAPTER 52

Sarah was on her feet, her cane clattering to the floor. She'd heard Miranda's clear voice ringing from the audience, "That's him! That's him!" And she knew: I'm the one he's after.

Rachel, at the table beside her, gasped. Sarah had gotten so used to blackness, it took her a moment to gather her thoughts to rip off her glasses. She still couldn't see! She'd forgotten, she'd taped her eyes shut so she'd really be blind. Where was her cane? She needed a weapon. He was coming for her. She heard a crash, knew it was the front bistro table hitting the floor. He must have moved past Sommes and Margery. Why didn't Sommes hit him, trip him, do something?

She ripped at the tape, feeling eyelashes and bits of skin come with it as she jerked and scratched at the damned adhesive. Her eyes blurred and watered blinking into the lights of the now brightly lit stage. Yellow polka dots danced before her. She moved her foot around, searching for the cane. Fatal to bend down, to lose blurry sight of the sparkling spots and gleaming scythe swimming toward her.

"Before my body, I throw my warlike shield. Lay on, Macduff," he screamed.

Sarah's frantic foot found the cane. She swerved to the

left to avoid the glistening blade coming at her, bent for her weapon, straightened and swung it, as Bernhardt would have, like the sword of Jeanne d'Arc.

"Let fall thy blade," the maniac sneered, ducking her first swing. "I bear a charmed life."

It hit her like a blow to the chest. Macbeth's death scene! He thinks he's the murderous king. Intends to kill me! Sarah planted her feet, gritted her teeth, took aim, and swung her cane again, polka dots swimming before her eyes. She swung at the candy man, the battered briefcase, the deerstalker's hat. This creep had tried to wreck her life, wreck this show, harm Miranda.

The blow caught him on the left leg and sent him sprawling into the bistro table she and Rachel had just vacated, his weapon clattering to the floor. On her knees from the force of her swing, Sarah looked around and swarming police were on top of the maniac. Gomez, as fast as *les flics*, was already in the mix, his shouting adding to the chaos.

"*Magnifique, Mademoiselle,*" Mary's detective said pulling Sarah to her feet and handcuffs from his back pocket. "You and *la petite* have made good work."

"Who is he?" Sarah hissed, as Vidal hauled up the lunatic — babbling something about Princess Diana buried with Americans — and cuffed him. "I think he sent me a poem."

"*Bien sûr,*" Vidal replied. "Messieurs John and Ben *explique* from the picture you send with your mobile. Is the same as in the poem book from London."

CHAPTER 53

So here he was again. Talk about *déjà vu*. John was opening more wine bottles looking out at Paris rooftops from his kitchen window, his apartment full of friends, police, cast members, and other hangers-on. Another murder solved.

The only thing still missing was Miranda prancing around in her Lady Gaga T-shirt bragging about her detective skills. A bittersweet occasion — the cast was leaving Paris. *Don't Look Now* was already booked for a West End tour then on to Broadway. The producers were ecstatic with the publicity from all the killings. It was only September, and advance ticket sales had the show booked almost to Christmas.

As much as John complained about the never-ending chaos with Sarah in residence, he adored having her. His life would be decidedly dull with her gone. It made him want to cry. He hadn't felt that in a long time!

He picked up several aerated bottles, Bisquit clicking along at his heels, and headed for the noisy chatter of the dining room where an abundance of cheese and spreads loaded down the grand table overhung by its glitzy Murano glass chandelier. A full bar was set up on the buffet along the wall.

Detective Vidal was explaining to Sarah and several others that the murderer-stalker was, indeed, a fellow actor as they had surmised. Name of James Powell. Dropped from a show that Sarah had ultimately played in.

"Ah, he knew the workings of backstage," Sommes said. "And, of course, he'd seen the film. Understood the visual impact of the red slicker."

John set down his bottles hard. "I don't get it. If this Powell fellow was gone from the show before Sarah even arrived, what was his gripe against her?"

Vidal shrugged, a weary sag momentarily collapsing his face. "Is complicated. Always so with disorders of the mind."

Conversation stopped, all eyes turned toward the detective. He squared his shoulders and briefly outlined what police inquisitors had so far determined about the guy Sarah had dubbed the Man in Disguise. Powell had somehow turned a long simmering grief over Princess Diana's death into smoldering hatred against Americans when he discovered through burglarizing Sarah's apartment that the poem read at the royal's funeral was written by a Yank.

"He first was made angry," Vidal explained, "when Mademoiselle Sarah was elected to play Lady Macbeth. Such a thing was unfair, he told investigators, because he was a properly schooled Englishman who had been ejected from his role in the same play."

So, the detective went on, Powell set out to harass Sarah while she was in London, snatching her purse, breaking into her flat. It was when he found the van Dyke book there that he found the source of poem read at the Princess Diana's funeral. Sarah, another beautiful blonde, then became the focus of Powell's twisted logic.

"Of course," Sommes snapped, hitting himself in the head in apparent exasperation. "I do remember the bloke now. A show I was in many years ago, he had a minor part, but always putting on airs about his classical training. And an obsession with the Royal Family. Thought rather well of himself. But quite a nobody, really. So that's why he seemed vaguely familiar when I saw him in that awful thing on Gaité Street."

"Explain then," John said addressing Vidal, "what any of this had to do with the murder of the first actress in the role of the psychic?"

"Only to confuse," Vidal replied. "Powell read of it in English *journaux* and obtained *l'idée* to kill the second actress to obscure his plan to murder Mademoiselle Sarah. But first, he send her all the flowers to bedevil her. How you say, stalk, in English."

"Makes a sick kind of sense in a warped mind," Sarah said. "Constantly changing disguises, a way to taunt other actors. Show he could play any character, get in your face and you wouldn't recognize him. I gotta give him credit, he was good. But what about the ashes?"

Vidal smiled. "The only good news. From wood, not human."

"Nonetheless, absurdly awful," Rachel said. "And the lighting man? Wrong place at the wrong time?"

"He worked for some little period in London," Vidal said. "Perhaps he recognize the killer."

Pierre, who had been listening intently, interrupted. "It is to say, Mademoiselle Sarah was targeted only because *Américaine?*"

"Oui, exactement," Vidal replied.

"I do not think you should go from Paris," Pierre said, turning to Sarah. "You have done much here, and your French it is better." He gave her a sly wink and an ever so slight faux punch with his elbow. "I 'ave say I will help to find the work. You 'ave much talent to be the show alone."

John brightened at the suggestion. "There has been quite a lot of English-speaking theater here lately. What a grand idea."

"I'd love it," Sarah said. "I dread leaving Vicki and Miranda. But I have to work. And this California bunch of producers seems to have big bucks and bigger plans for West End and Broadway."

Those gathered heaved a collective sigh, moved toward the bar, reached for cheese.

Ben spoke up. "I not to understand about the *pompier.* The, how you say, culprit followed very closely with Rochegrosse's *ouvre. Qu'est que c'est?"*

Vidal shook his head. "The doctors 'ave say he sees himself the chaste knight in Rochegrosse painting of *le chevalier* among the virgins. *Le chevalier* was hanging in d'Orsay for some small period. But no evidence that Powell devote much time in Paris until he begins to stalk Mademoiselle Sarah. He encounter with the seamstress someplace, perhaps here, perhaps London. She may have left Paris with him, and he aids her to find sewing jobs with *théâtres* he plays in." Vidal raised an eyebrow. "Difficult to say. We found in his room ladies' silver shoes that he perhaps wears."

"My shoes, my extravagant shoes? He wore them?" Sarah moaned. "I hope you burned them!"

"I said before," Mary finally chimed in, "that the guy had some strange fantasies. So many of his posters, or whatever you call them, had women in very weird kinds of peril. By the way, where in the world is the kid detective? Can't believe she's not here celebrating."

Sarah frowned. "Vicki was picking her up at school. They were going to interview a new babysitter."

"Ah, I'm sorry to hear that," Mary said. "I know that's hard on you."

"I'm pretty miserable. I think Miranda is, too," Sarah said.

"*C'est vrai,*" Pierre said. "You must not to go. I will introduce to you *une directeur* who has *théâtre* here."

Bisquit suddenly set up a howl, even before the knock on the door. John opened it to Miranda and Vicki.

Sarah's heart nearly stopped. Her niece was wearing a red mackintosh!

"Miranda," she screamed, "take that horrid thing off!"

The room went silent.

Miranda eyed her aunt coolly. "It's always been mine. Daddy sent it."

Vicki, standing behind the child, caught Sarah's eye and pointed her thumb at herself.

Sarah took a deep, steadying breath. "So your mom thinks it's okay?"

"Sure," Miranda answered, her tone still cool and standoffish. "She's the one who found the package when it came."

"Ah. So how did the interview go?" Sarah ventured.

"I don't like her," Miranda said, making a face.

"We can't go on like this forever," Vicki snapped. "That's the third one this week. I was hoping that raincoat would make you happy."

"I spoke to Adeel. Maybe that will perk you up," Sarah said to Miranda.

She frowned and gave her aunt a sidelong look. "Does he know I got him sprung?"

"Um, well… I told him you were so concerned about him that you went to the police station."

Miranda wheeled on her mother. "I told you! I told you! I want Aunt Sarah. We're a team."

"I know, baby," said Sarah, tearing up, throwing her arms wide to reach out to Miranda.

"I'm not a baby. I'm a detective." Miranda stomped her foot. "I've solved murders."

Sarah started to laugh.

"It's not funny. You can't leave."

"Sorry," Sarah said. "It's just a thrill to see you back in form, back to your old self." She threw her arms wide again with a grin even wider. "Come on, BABY, give me a hug."

CHAPTER 54

Sarah had Pierre along this time, waiting in her usual spot on the sidewalk for Miranda to come charging out of school.

And here she came, bounding along, dragging that impossibly heavy satchel. "Why," Sarah asked Pierre, "are little kids expected to carry such big book bags?"

Pierre shrugged. "Same always."

Ah. Was she never going to get used to French ways? Why would any sane person voluntarily choose to live here? Things were so much easier, made so much more sense, in California!

Miranda skidded up. "Okay, I'm ready. *Allons-y*."

"Well, I'm learning some French. 'Let's go.' Right?" Sarah queried.

Miranda reached for her hand. "*Oui*, Aunt Sarah. You're a good student. Now let's go meet your new boss."

"Don't get ahead of yourself, smart aleck. She only said she would consider Pierre's proposal for a play in English."

Sarah tousled her niece's hair. "And with the projection you displayed yelling about the Man in Disguise, you'll probably be joining me on the stage sometime soon."

"What's projection?" Miranda asked.